Unusual Christmas Occurrences

MARK EDWARD TATE

UNUSUAL CHRISTMAS OCCURRENCES

CONTENTS

THE VENOMOUS TREE

It was the coldest December they could remember. The McAllister household was buzzing with the kind of excitement that only the holiday season could bring. Jack McAllister, the family man with a knack for his Christmas cheer, was putting the finishing touches on the tree when a sudden sharp sting pierced his hand. He glanced down, his heart sinking as he spotted a tiny spider scurrying away. "Just a little bite," he muttered, shaking it off, but the swelling began almost immediately.

By the time his wife, Sarah, noticed the growing redness around his wrist, Jack's hand resembled a balloon. "You need to see a doctor," she insisted, her voice laced with concern. Their older child, their daughter, Emma, nodded solemnly, her wide eyes mirroring her mother's fear.

At the hospital, the doctors worked quickly, administering antibiotics and monitoring the infection. Jack felt groggy but relieved when they finally sent him home, armed with medication and a stern warning to keep the area clean. "Just a little holiday scare," he joked weakly, trying to lighten the mood. Sarah and Emma exchanged glances, but he could see the worry on their faces.

Days passed, and the infection subsided, but Jack's mind felt heavy. He wanted nothing more than to be a good father to Emma and his younger child, especially little Benny, who was full of energy and curiosity.

The next Saturday morning, Jack decided to take Benny to the zoo, hoping the outing would shake o the lingering unease. Benny had been very upset when he learned that his father had gotten bitten by a spider. The thought that his daddy might be seriously hurt had shaken him badly.

As they wandered through the exhibits, Benny's laughter echoed in the air, and Jack felt a sense of normalcy returning. They marveled at the elephants, giggled at the monkeys, and watched in awe as the jaguars prowled gracefully in their enclosure. Jack felt a warm glow of happiness, until suddenly, a dark cloud rolled in.

He blinked, and in an instant, the world around him shifted. In his nightmarish vision, Benny slipped through the railing and fell into the jaguar enclosure. The sleek, spotted cats turned their piercing eyes on his son, primal hunger igniting within them. Jack's heart raced as he screamed, but the sound was swallowed by the roar of the animals. He tried to step forward, desperate to save Benny, but it was as if he were encased in molasses, unable to move closer.

Just as the jaguars lunged forward, sharp claws outstretched, Jack felt a small hand shake him awake.

His eyes shot open, and he found himself sitting on a bench, breathing heavily, the sun shining brightly above. Benny was looking at him, his innocent face filled with concern. "Daddy? Are you okay?"

Jack pulled his son into a tight embrace, his heart still racing from the remnants of the nightmare. "I'm fine, buddy. Just a bad dream," he whispered, feeling the warmth of his son's small body against him, grounding him in reality.

"How can you dream during the day? Did the jaguars scare you?" Benny asked, his eyes wide with curiosity.

Jack chuckled nervously, ruing his son's hair. "They're just big kitties, right? Nothing to be scared of. I guess I'm still a little groggy, out of it from the hospital." He held Benny's hand tightly as they moved away from the 6 jaguar exhibit, thankful for the solid connection between them.

-2-

The day after their trip to the zoo, Jack felt a sense of dread creeping back into his mind. Despite his efforts to shake off the incident at the zoo, he couldn't help but feel that shadows lingered just beneath the surface.

He decided to take Sarah Christmas shopping at the local mall. She had been looking forward to it, and he hoped it would be a fun way to celebrate the season together.

As they strolled through the brightly decorated mall, the atmosphere was electric with holiday spirit, twinkling lights, festive music, and the scent of peppermint floating through the air. Jack and Sarah laughed as they browsed through the stores, picking out gifts and treats for their kids. Everything felt perfect, and yet, the nagging sense of something bad was about to happen, remained.

They stepped into a bookstore, the warm glow of the lights and the smell of freshly printed pages wrapping around them like a cozy blanket. Jack leaned on a shelf, flipping through a book, when suddenly, a chill ran down his spine. He looked up to see two men in hoodies standing just outside the store, their faces obscured, their bodies tense. An unsettling feeling gripped him, but he shook his head, forcing himself to focus on Sarah. No! This isn't real. This isn't happening again, please no!

Without warning, the scene morphed. He was no longer in the bookstore but trapped in another daytime nightmare. The two faceless men were now inside the store, and they were coming for him and Sarah. Jack grabbed her hand, pulling her toward the exit that lead into the mall. The mall seemed to stretch endlessly, each turn leading them deeper into chaos. The sound of the two faceless men's footsteps echoed behind them, growing louder as they dashed through the food court, weaving past startled shoppers.

"Jack! What's happening?" Sarah gasped, her voice strained, but all he could do was urge her to run faster. The faceless men were relentless, their shadows looming ever closer.

They burst into the bookstore again, desperately searching for a way out, but before Jack could even think, he felt a sharp pain in his chest. The two men had pulled out guns, and he could see the glint of metal as they pointed them at Sarah and him. He opened his mouth to shout, to warn her, but the sound never escaped. Just as the shots rang out, everything went black.

Jack jolted awake, gasping for air, drenched in sweat. Somehow they were back in their car in the parking lot. He quickly turned to Sarah, who was behind the wheel, her grip tight twisting the wheel up and down. She was pale, her eyes wide, but she wouldn't meet his gaze. The silence in the car was deafening.

"Sarah?" He murmured, his heart racing from the remnants of the nightmare, or whatever it was. "Are you okay?"

She took a deep breath, her eyes still fixed on the road ahead. "We're fine, Jack," she said finally, her voice low and at. "But we are never going to talk about this again."

Confusion washed over him. "What do you mean? Talk about what?"

Her silence was a heavy weight that filled the car. He could see her jaw clenching, the way her knuckles turned white from the pressure of holding on the wheel. It was as if a wall had gone up between them, and he felt himself slipping away, caught between the echoes of his daytime nightmare and the reality of their situation.

"Sarah, please," he urged, trying to reach out to her. "If something's wrong, I need to know."

She finally glanced at him, her eyes betraying a mixture of fear and anger. "Jack, we're going home. Let me just focus on getting us home, okay?"

The tension in the car was so high, and Jack could feel his heart sinking. He wanted to reassure her, to tell her that it was just a dream, but the words stuck in his throat. Instead, they drove in silence, the world outside the car was blurred by the haze of his anxiety.

When they finally arrived home, the warmth of their house felt cold and distant. Jack stepped inside, his mind racing with thoughts of the nightmare and Sarah's cryptic words. He wanted to protect his family from fear, but how could he do that when he himself felt so shaken?

As he watched Sarah walk into the kitchen, lost in her own thoughts, Jack realized that perhaps some battles were meant to be fought alone. He would keep the darkness at bay for their sake, but deep inside, he knew he had to confront his own fears before they spiraled out of control.

With a heavy heart, he joined Sarah in the kitchen, determined to find a way to bridge the silence that had begun to grow between them. After all, the holiday season was meant for light, and he would do everything he could to bring that light back into their home.

The sun shone brightly the next day, casting a warm glow over the McAllister backyard. Jack felt lighter, as if the weight of the previous nightmares had finally begun to lift. The infection in his hand had healed, and he was determined to make the most of the day with his family. He donned his swim trunks and joined his kids in the pool, their laughter echoing around them as they tossed around colorful Nerf balls over a net in the center of the pool.

Jack felt invigorated as he dove into the cool water, splashing around with Benny and Emma. They played games, laughing as they threw the balls back and forth, the joy of the moment washing away any lingering shadows. For a brief time, he relished the normalcy of family life, the worries fading like ripples in the water.

But just as he was about to catch a ball thrown by Emma, something shifted. The sunlight seemed to flicker, and the water around him darkened ominously. Jack's heart raced as he looked down, spotting a n cutting through the murky depths. Panic surged through him as the realization there was a shark in the pool and it was circling them.

"Get out! Get out!" Jack shouted, his voice a mix of fear and urgency. But the kids were frozen, staring wide-eyed at the dark water. Just as the great white shark burst from the depths, jaws wide open, Jack felt a rush of water engulf him, as if a giant wave had appeared in front of him to block his path from saving his kids.

He awoke, sputtering and gasping as though he had just emerged from the depths of the ocean. Drenched in sweat, he sat up in bed, his heart pounding fiercely. The room swam around him, and a wave of disorientation washed over him.

"Jack?" Sarah's voice cut through the haze, her expression filled with concern. She was standing at the foot of the bed, her eyes wide as she pointed toward his ankle. "We found another bite mark! They either missed it at the hospital or you've been bitten again!"

Jack looked down to see a swollen, angry bite mark on his ankle, the same kind of bite that had plagued his hand days before. Panic set in. "Sarah, it hurts!" he exclaimed. The pain had rushed in once he had taken notice of it.

Without missing a beat, Sarah rushed to the phone, her fingers trembling as she called for help. Soon, the sound of sirens filled the air, and Jack was being wheeled out of the house on a stretcher, his family trailing behind, their faces painted with worry.

-3-

In the ambulance, Jack tried to catch his breath, but the anxiety from the nightmare was clung to him. As they arrived at the emergency room, he was wheeled through the busy halls, the fluorescent lights buzzing overhead. Just as they rolled him into the elevator, the doors slid shut, and the lights flickered ominously. Suddenly, Jack felt a strange sensation, as if the elevator was falling upward.

"Is this normal?" he gasped, looking at the paramedic beside him, who shrugged, looking equally bewildered.

Then everything went black.

When he opened his eyes again, Jack found himself in a hospital room, surrounded by the familiar faces of his wife, kids, and extended family. Relief washed over him, and he tried to sit up, but quickly laid back down.

"Jack! You scared us!" Emma exclaimed, rushing to his side, her worry transforming into relief.

"Are you okay, Daddy?" Benny's small voice squeaked from behind Sarah.

"I'm okay, buddy," Jack smiled, though his mind was still racing. "Just a little bump in the road."

Suddenly, the atmosphere shifted as a figure appeared in the doorway. Jack squinted, and his heart skipped a beat. Standing there, holding a bright red balloon, was none other than Stephen King, his favorite author.

"I think I have the right room?" King said, his voice low and playful. "I was told someone named Jack was having a birthday party and I had an extra balloon.." With that, he gave a friendly wave and turned to leave with the balloon floating in front of the doorway.

Jack's family turned to look at the iconic author, mouths agape, before they burst into laughter. The tension in the room broke, and Jack couldn't help but chuckle himself, the absurdity of the moment bringing warmth to his heart.

Now that's a nightmare I'd gladly wake up from," he said, looking at his family, who were still giggling at King's unexpected visit.

He squeezed his family's hands, grateful for their presence and the joy that filled the room, knowing that together, they could face anything life threw at them.

"Did they make sure I don't have anymore of these bites on my body?" He asked.

"We hired a spider control company to clear out the house. They found a huge nest in the middle of the Christmas Tree unfortunately, I really loved that tree, but they took it away. I think the coast is clear. Rest up honey, I'm taking the kids downstairs for breakfast, then we'll return this afternoon to pick you up."

"I love you all so much." Tears began to form in his eyes. " I know how much you loved that tree, we'll get another one I promise. That one was venomous!"

INTO THE HOUSE

Bill settled into his worn leather armchair, the crackling embers of the fireplace casting a warm glow across the room. He took a deep sip of bourbon, savoring the rich flavor as he watched the flames dance. It was Christmas Eve, and the soft sound of snowflakes tapping against the window seemed to harmonize with the comforting silence of his home.

As he swirled the amber liquid in his glass, there was a knock at the door, breaking the tranquility. Bill set his drink down, walked to the front door, and opened it to reveal his postman, a young man in a thick winter coat, his cheeks flushed from the cold.

"Evening, Mr. Bill!" The postman said, smiling brightly. "Just delivering the last of the holiday mail. You're my last stop for the day!"

"Come in, come in!" Bill waved him inside, gesturing toward the fire. "You must be freezing out there."

The postman hesitated for a moment, then stepped over the threshold, grateful for the warmth.

He removed his cap, revealing tousled hair, and took a seat across from Bill. "Thanks! It's a bit brisk out today!"

Bill took another sip of his bourbon, feeling a story bubbling up from within. He leaned forward, the firelight illuminating the lines of his weathered face. "You know, this reminds me of a Christmas many years ago, the day I met my wife."

The postman raised an eyebrow, intrigued. "Really? I'd love to hear it." He removed his gloves and held the palms of his hands towards the fireplace.

Bill smiled, his eyes brightly lit up with nostalgia. "It was a Christmas Eve just like this. I had had gone to the mall to pick up a few last-minute gifts. The place was packed, people running around all about. Everyone seemed rushed, in a hurry. As I was leaving the mall, walking towards my car in the parking lot, I saw this beautiful young woman, my wife-to-be! She was carrying quite the load, she was struggling with all her bags. I remember she had this beautiful red scarf wrapped around her neck. I didn't usually go for blondes, but man let me tell you she was a knock out! A ten out of ten! She had me mesmerized! I couldn't take my eyes off her!"

The postman leaned in, captivated. "What happened next?"

"Well," Bill continued, "as she was trying to juggle her purchases, a thief came running up from behind her and snatched her purse from her side. I saw it all unfold in slow motion. She fell to the ground, bags falling and spilling out Christmas gifts everywhere on the ground. The thief sprinted away with her purse leaving her bleeding on the ground. Without thinking, I took off after him."

The postman's eyes widened. "Did you catch him?"

"Not quite," Bill chuckled, shaking his head. "But I did manage to catch up to him and trip him as he was making his escape. The guy went flying, and somehow I landed right on top of him. We wrestled for a moment and I was able to get him into a solid chokehold. I just hung on to him as tight as I could until security arrived. They took custody of him and walked her stolen purse back to her. She gave me the warmest hug I had ever received in my life."

"Wow, that's heroic!" The postman exclaimed, his admiration palpable.

Bill grinned, his hear warming at the memory. "When the dust settled, there she was, looking at me with those big, grateful eyes. She took me out to lunch after. I escorted her to another mall where she finished up her holiday shopping. Afterwards, she invited me to her house. We talked for hours that night. As she walked me to the front door to say goodnight, she kissed me. I'll never forget that first kiss. Amazing. She called me he knight in shining armor! She asked me to take her to the movies on Christmas Day! The funny part, is I still have no earthly idea what movie we saw! The rest, as they say, is history."

The postman smiled, visibly moved. "That's an incredible story, Mr. Bill. You really saved Christmas for her."

"More than that, I think." Bill said, his voice softening. "She saved me. I was a lonely man before that day. Meeting her changed everything. Unfortunately, the thief that robbed her escaped security just before the police arrived. He apparently robbed six other women that Christmas. One of the women was seriously injured. They never caught the bastard!"

A moment of silence hung between them, the warmth of the fire enveloping them both. The postman, still processing the tale, glanced around the cozy room, filled with memories and love.

"Thank you for sharing that," He finally said. "I didn't know you had such an amazing story behind your life." Bill chuckled again, taking another sip of his bourbon.

"Well, not many do. But there's more to the story if you've got another minute or two to spare for an old babbling man?"

"Definitely." The postman responded.

"I told you that one of those women he robbed that holiday season was hurt bad right?" Bill continued.

"Yes." The postman seemed very interested in hearing more details.

"My wife. There were no signs of trauma, other than mentally shaken up at first."

"What? No! What happened?"

"We enjoyed Christmas together. Saw a movie, delivered our presents the day after to our family members and friends together. We were inseparable after that horrific incident it seems. But..." Bill paused, poured himself a double shot of bourbon in his glass from the bottle sitting next to him on the side table. He took a sip as he sat back in his chair remembering.

"What happened Mr. Bill?" The postman asked eager to hear the rest of Bill's story.

"Apparently, at some point during the struggle, when she had fallen to the ground, she was injured badly, and didn't know it."

"I thought you guys were okay after the incident. You said she took you out to lunch, you spent Christmas together, sounded like a match made in heaven, love at first sight, what on earth happened? Please continue!"

"Everything did seem perfect, at first. An entire month passed by, a perfect month. Then the headaches came. She began to feel a lot of pain in her neck and shoulders. She began feeling numbness and tingling in her legs. I took her to the hospital right away! She had broken bones, internal bleeding. Short end of it is she lost the ability to walk. Paralyzed from the waist down for the rest of her life."

"Mr. Bill, I...I don't know what to say. That's terrible. I mean that's one true love story if I've ever heard one, but that

went dark fast!" The postman had begun to feel a little uneasy, restless in his chair. "I hate to ask you this, but do you mind if I use your restroom Mr. Bill?"

"Yes, over to the kitchen, then down the hallway, first door on your left." Bill was lost momentarily in his memories. The postman stood up and disappeared into the hallway.

Bill downed the rest of his drink and set the glass on the coffee table in front of him. He reached down into the side of his chair and pulled out a hunting knife secured in its leather sheath. He unsnapped the fastener holding its handle and pulled the knife out holding it in front of him. The flames from the fire danced their reflections on its blade.

Bill stood up and walked to the kitchen, then turned and started down the hallway. He stopped. He turned towards the bathroom door. He heard the toilet flushing. He tightened his grip on the handle of the knife.

Inside the bathroom, the postman washed his hands in the sink and then dried them off with a towel hanging from the shower rod, he turned and opened the door. Mr. Bill was waiting outside. He had zero time to react.

The postman staggered back into the bathroom, eyes wide with shock and pain. He clutched his stomach, where the blade had pierced through his shirt, blood seeping through his fingers. "What...what have you done?" He gasped, disbelief etched across his face.

Bill's expression was cold, a mix of anger and resolve. "You thought you'd get away with it, didn't you? You thought nobody would find you! I know the truth! You robbed my wife, you hurt her bad, and now you will pay for it!"

The postman dropped to his knees, his breath coming in ragged gasps as he struggled to process what was happening to him. "Please...I don't know what you're talking about...you...you stabbed me Mr. Bill!" He stammered, trying to stand up, failing as his own body betrayed him.

Bill's voice low and steady, "You crossed a line, Mr. Postman. You should have thought about the consequences before you laid hands on my wife!" Bill knelt down on a knee putting himself at the postman's level. The postman's eyes were rapidly darting around for any escape, but there was none to be found.

The postman's strength began to wane, his thoughts raced. He could feel the cold grip of fear wrapping around him like a vice. "Wait...we can talk about this..." words were hard to form, he wanted to plead for his life, desperation creeping in. "It wasn't personal! I needed money! Just a mistake!"

Bill shook his head violently back and forth, his heart pounding with a mix of adrenaline and grief. "There's no talking your way out of this. You've made your choices, and now you must face them head on!"

The postman felt the world around him start to fade, the pain blurring his vision. He gasped for breath, the reality of his situation was crashing down like a tidal wave. He was going to die! No one could save him. In his final moments, he realized the truth in Bill's words, there was no escaping the consequences of his actions.

Bill stood over the postman watching him bleed out. Watching as he took his last breath. "It's taken me a long, long time to track you down! Track you down I did! I interviewed all the victims, innocent women, all the witnesses I could find in those police reports! I was ready to give up, thought I'd never find you. Every promising lead I got just brought me to another lead to nowhere. I would've given up, that is until I met with a young woman named, Emily. She had been the only witness to see anything of value.

Emily was the daughter of one of your victims that somehow never got interviewed by the police. About a week after her mother was robbed she told her mother she had seen the guy that robbed her. Only, the guy was wearing a postman's uniform, delivering a package to her neighbor's house.

Emily had been getting her mail out of her mailbox at the end of her driveway. She saw the postman walking back to his truck. He waved to her. He gave her a warm smile. She had been there when her mother had been robbed, at the mall. She had been only feet behind her mother when her mother's assailant came up and snatched her purse away from her. The robber, YOU, ran away like a coward that you are but you screwed up didn't you! You turned around just long enough for Emily to get a good look at you!

After she told her mom that the postman was her robber, her mom wouldn't believe it. Her mom actually convinced Emily there was no way their postman was the man that robbed her! Can you believe that? Her mom never reported this information to the police!"

A few moments later Bill called out to his wife who had been hiding in their bedroom the entire time, "Coast is clear honey! Come on out! The bastard's dead!"

The bedroom door creaked open. Bill's wife rolled out into the hallway in her wheelchair. She rolled up to Bill's side at the bathroom door. The two of them stayed silent for the next couple of minutes staring at the dead man's body on their bathroom floor. His wife took him by the hand, gave it a little squeeze, then held it to her lips, she kissed the palm of his hand softly.

"Merry Christmas baby! Ho, ho, ho!" Bill shouted hysterically like a mad man in his best Santa Claus impression.

"Merry Christmas to you babe! Let's go celebrate in the living room shall we? You did leave me at least one glass of bourbon didn't you?"

"Yes ma'am!"

MERRY LITTLE PRANKSTERS

It was Christmas Eve, and as snowflakes danced lazily from the sky, Jake, a dedicated delivery man, navigated through the winter wonderland, his truck loaded with packages destined for the next neighborhood. For Jake, it was a labor of love. Each box in his truck contained gifts that would bring joy to families across town.

However, this year, two particularly mischievous boys, Tommy and Billy, had decided to make it their mission to turn Jake's shift into a nightmare. Dubbed the "Prankster Twins" by the locals, these two were known for their devilish antics and relentless determination to stir up trouble.

As Jake pulled up to his first stop in the neighborhood, he spotted the boys lurking behind a snowbank, their eyes sparkling with mischief. "Here we go," he muttered, shaking his head. He stepped out of the truck, only to have a snowball whiz past his ear. It splattered against the side of his vehicle, and he turned, his expression a mix of annoyance and disbelief.

"Hey! Cut it out!" He shouted, but Tommy and Billy only giggled and crouched behind their snowy fortress, readying another round of projectiles.

Jake sighed, knowing he had to get the packages delivered. He walked briskly to the front door, hoping to ignore the chaos behind him. Just as he rang the doorbell, he heard the unmistakable sound of laughter and the crunch of snow. He turned to see the twins charging toward him, armed with snowballs.

"Look out, Jake!" Tommy shouted, launching a flurry of snow at him. The first hit him square in the chest, and he stumbled back, half-laughing, half-fuming.

"Seriously, guys!" Jake exclaimed, wiping the snow from his jacket. He could feel his patience wearing thin. "I'm just trying to do my job here!"

"Job?" Billy taunted, tossing another snowball that landed harmlessly on the ground. "You mean delivering presents? You can't deliver here their on the naughty list!"

With a resigned grin, Jake picked up a handful of snow and packed it tightly. "Alright, you little rascals, two can play at this game." He hurled the snowball, which caught Tommy off guard and splattered against his face. The boys erupted in laughter, momentarily forgetting their mission.

"Really?" Jake groaned, unable to suppress a laugh despite the chaos. "You guys are relentless!"

"Only because it's Christmas Eve!" Billy shouted, his eyes gleaming with mischief. "Santa needs to know you're ready for a real challenge!"

With a half-smile, Jake took a deep breath. He knew he had to finish his deliveries, but perhaps there was a way to turn the tables. "Alright, boys. How about a deal? You help me with the last few packages, and I'll give you a little surprise."

Their eyes widened with curiosity, and the boys exchanged glances, momentarily distracted from their pranks. "What kind of surprise?" Tommy asked, his interest piqued.

"A special Christmas treat, cookies and hot chocolate at the end of the route, and a five dollar bill for each of you." Jake replied, grinning. "But only if you promise to behave!"

After a moment of discussion, the twins finally agreed, and Jake set them to work. Together, they trudged through the snow, delivering packages while the boys tried (and hilariously failed) to rein in their pranks. Instead of snowballs, they threw in cheers and laughter, and Jake couldn't help but feel the holiday spirit lifting his heart.

By the time they finished, the sun was setting, casting a golden glow over the snow-covered streets. Jake led the boys back to his truck, and as promised, he produced a thermos of hot cocoa and a tin of freshly baked cookies. He pulled out his wallet and presented them each with a five dollar bill.

"Alright, you two," He said, pouring the steaming chocolate into cups. "You earned it, after all, every delivery man needs a little help from his friends."

As they sipped their cocoa and munched on cookies, Jake realized that despite the chaos, he wouldn't trade this Christmas Eve for anything. The laughter of the twins filled the air, and he knew that even pranksters could bring a little magic to the season.

-2-

As the warmth of the cocoa settled in their bellies, Jake felt a sense of camaraderie with Tommy and Billy, the once-annoying pranksters now transformed into eager little helpers. But as they finished their treats and the sun dipped lower in the sky, the boys exchanged glances, and a mischievous shine returned to their eyes.

"Hey, Jake," Billy said, leaning closer with a conspiratorial whisper, "what if we made this delivery job even more fun?"

Jake, still riding the high of their earlier teamwork, raised an eyebrow. "What do you mean by fun'?"

"Like, what if we gave the packages a little... twist?" Tommy suggested, a wicked smile spreading across his face. "You know, make things exciting!"

Before Jake could respond, the twins sprang into action. They began to rearrange the packages, swapping labels and mixing up the contents. Jake's heart sank as he realized what they were doing.

"No, no! You can't do that!" He exclaimed, rushing toward them. "Those packages are for families! They need to get to the right places!"

"Oh, come on, Jake! Don't be such a Grinch!" Billy shot back, giggling as he threw a random package at the snowbank, where it landed with a soft thud. "It'll be hilarious! Just think of the chaos!"

Jake felt a wave of frustration wash over him. "This isn't a joke! People are counting on these gifts!"

One of them went flying through the air, landing just short of a snowbank where it burst open, revealing a shower of colorful wrapping paper and a soccer ball that rolled into the street.

"See? Fun!" Tommy shouted.

"Guys, stop!" Jake pleaded, his voice rising in urgency. But the boys were no longer listening. They were caught up in their own game, reveling in the pandemonium they had created.

Jake felt a knot tightening in his stomach. He had to regain control before things spiraled completely out of hand. "Alright, listen up!" he shouted, his voice cutting through their laughter. "You two need to help me clean this up right now! If you don't, I'll have to call your parents."

The twins paused, their expressions shifting from mischief to defiance. "You wouldn't!" Billy exclaimed, crossing his arms.

"Try me," Jake said firmly. "I'm serious!"

For a moment, the boys exchanged glances, weighing their options. Then, with a collective shrug, they decided to double down on their pranks. "Fine! You want us to clean up?" Tommy said, a devilish grin creeping back onto his face. "How about we make it a real mess first?"

Before Jake could react, they lunged into action, grabbing handfuls of snow and packing it tightly. They began launching snowballs at the remaining packages, giggling maniacally as they splattered them with snow. Jake's frustration turned to panic as he realized just how far they were willing to go. "Stop!" he shouted, rushing toward them, but not before a barrage of snowballs hit him square in the chest. It was like being caught in a winter storm of mischief, and as he stumbled back, he felt a mix of anger and disbelief at how quickly their playful energy had turned mean-spirited.

"Let's see how many we can ruin!" Billy cackled, and Jake watched in horror as they continued their rampage, tossing packages and burying them in snow.

"Enough! That's it!" Jake shouted, his patience finally snapped. He took a deep breath, forcing himself to remain calm. "If you don't stop right now, I'll be reporting you to your parents. Or I'll be forced to call the police! This is getting out of hand!"

At the mention of their parents and the police being called, the boys paused, uncertainty flickering in their eyes. But instead of backing down, they just exchanged sly smiles. "You think we're scared?" Tommy said defiantly. "You're just a delivery guy! No one will believe you!"

With that, they sprang into action again, this time grabbing handfuls of snow and shoving them down the back of Jake's coat. The shock of the cold made him yelp, and he spun around to face them, eyes wide with disbelief.

"You little bast..." He started, but before he could finish, the boys erupted into laughter, their cackles filling the air.

In that moment, something shifted inside Jake. He looked at the two boys, who were now caught up in their own little world of chaos, and an idea sparked in his mind. If they were going to act like this, maybe he could outsmart them instead of letting them get the better of him.

"Alright, you two," He said, a grin slowly creeping across his face. "If you want to play like that, how about a challenge? Let's see who can clean up the most packages in the next ten minutes. If you win, I won't call your parents. But if I win, you have to help me deliver the rest of these packages properly."

Tommy and Billy glanced at each other, intrigued by the wager. "Deal!" They shouted in unison.

With that, Jake sprang into action, grabbing a few packages and tossing them into the truck. The boys, sensing the competition, followed suit but not without tossing in a few extra snowballs at Jake as he worked.

As the timer ticked down, the trio worked frantically, laughter and shouts filling the air as they raced against the clock. In the end, it was a close call, but Jake managed to gather more packages than the twins.

"Alright, I win!" He declared, panting and grinning. The boys, though disappointed, couldn't help but laugh at the absurdity of the situation.

"You're good at this, Jake," Tommy admitted, a hint of respect in his voice.

"Yeah, maybe we should team up more often," Billy added, giving Jake a playful shove.

With a chuckle, Jake replied, "Alright, how about this: let's finish the last few deliveries together, and I'll even throw in some extra cookies when we're done."

The boys exchanged glances and then nodded eagerly. Perhaps there was more to this Christmas Eve than pranks and mischief after all.

-3-

As Jake and the boys finished loading the last of the packages into the truck, the air crackled with excitement. The sun had dipped below the horizon, and the streetlights cast a warm glow over the snow-covered neighborhood. But as they prepared to set o on their final deliveries, Jake's patience was once again tested.

While he was busy checking o addresses on his delivery list, he caught Tommy and Billy plotting something in the corner of his eye. They had grabbed a handful of snow and were stung it down the side of one of the gift boxes. Jake turned just in time to see them pull out a small, shiny snow globe he had kept in the truck, a novelty item he had found at a thrift store. This snow globe was supposed to be a fun decoration, one that he had planned to give to his niece, but the boys saw it as a new target for their mischief.

"Hey! No! Not that!" Jake shouted, lunging forward as he watched them shake the globe, the glitter swirling inside like a wild winter storm.

But the twins, emboldened by their earlier antics, laughed and tossed the globe back and forth like a football. "What's it going to do? Does it grant wishes?" Billy taunted.

"Stop it!" Jake yelled, frustration boiling over. "You have no idea how important that is!"

The boys froze, a moment of silence hanging in the air, but it didn't last long. "What, you really think it's magical?" Tommy scoffed, rolling his eyes. "It's just a stupid snow globe."

Something inside Jake snapped. "You know what? Maybe it is magical! How about I promise you both that if you keep messing around, you'll end up trapped inside it forever? You'll both be looking out at the world while everyone else has fun!"

The twins exchanged glances, their expressions shifting from playful defiance to concern. "Yeah, right!"

Billy said, though there was a tremor in his voice. "No way that could really happen!"

"Try me!" Jake replied, his voice firm. "You think I'm joking? Keep it up, and I swear..."

But the twins, always seeking a thrill, decided to test the boundaries. "Fine! We dare you! Make that wish!" Tommy shouted, raising his hands dramatically, as if casting a spell.

Suddenly, the snow globe began to shimmer and shake violently in their hands. The glitter inside swirled faster and faster, a whirlwind of color and light. Jake's heart raced. "Wait! No! No Way!" He shouted, rushing forward, but it was too late.

With a blinding flash, a surge of energy erupted from the globe, Tommy and Billy vanished out of thin air in a brilliant light. Jake shielded his eyes, and when he opened them again, the boys were gone.

In their place, the snow globe hovered in mid-air, now glowing. Inside the globe, now miniaturized, Tommy and Billy appeared, their faces pressed against the glass, eyes wide with terror and disbelief. They were trapped, surrounded by swirling snowflakes that floated endlessly in their miniature world.

"Jake! Let us out! This isn't funny!" They cried, voices muffled as they banged their tiny fists against the glass. Their once sassy demeanor had vanished, replaced by panic.

Jake stood frozen, a mix of horror and guilt flooding his chest. "I didn't mean it! I was just trying to teach you a lesson!" He shouted, feeling helpless as he stared at their tiny faces.

"Please!" Tommy pleaded, his voice cracking. "We just wanted to have fun!"

With tears in their eyes, the boys turned to each other, realizing the weight of their choices. Now, they had nothing but the cold, glittering confines of the globe. Their cries echoed back at them, a haunting reminder of the mischief that had led them here.

"I just wanted you to understand that there are consequences to your actions." Jake shouted.

Jake knew he had to find a way to help the boys, as evil as they were. He took a deep breath and approached the globe, staring at the boys' faces, filled with a mixture of fear and desperation. "I'm going to fix this, I promise." He said, determination rising within him.

It was up to him to find a way to release the boys from their self-imposed prison, to teach them the value of humility, friendship, and the true meaning of the holiday spirit.

Jake set the snow globe down in the passenger seat of his truck. He had no idea how to reverse the wish, how to get those boys out of that globe. Part of him thought about just tossing the globe out into the snow bank, but he was a good man, it wasn't in his nature to be evil.

-4-

He decided to head to the local library, a place filled with old books and dusty tales. He hoped to find something, anything, that could help him understand the snow globe's magic and how to reverse its effects. The library was quiet, the only sound the soft crunch of his boots on the carpet as he approached the shelves.

After what felt like hours of searching, he stumbled upon a dusty old book titled "Wonders of the Enchanted: Artifacts and their Powers." With trembling hands, he opened it, flipping through pages filled with illustrations of magical items. It was there he found a section on wish-granting objects.

"Every wish carries a weight." He read aloud, his eyes scanning the text. "To undo a wish, one must understand the heart of the wisher. Only through selflessness and genuine remorse can the spell be broken."

Jake felt a utter of hope. "Selflessness and remorse." He muttered. He thought of Tommy and Billy, their mischievous pranks that had spiraled out of control. Perhaps they needed to understand the impact of their actions, not just on him, but on the people around them.

He decided to return to the snow globe, hoping that by showing genuine remorse for the boys' predicament and perhaps even showing them the joys of giving instead of taking, he could find a way to bring them back. He drove back to the neighborhood, the streets were glowing with Christmas lights.

When he arrived at the spot where the boys had first picked up the snow globe, Jake took a deep breath. He placed the globe on the hood of his truck and spoke to it softly, hoping the boys could hear him. "I'm sorry, Tommy and Billy. I didn't mean for things to go this far. You wanted to have fun, and I understand that. But you have to realize that every action has consequences."

Inside the globe, the boys' expressions softened, and they listened intently, their faces reflecting both fear and hope. "Jake, we're sorry too!" Tommy shouted, his voice muffled but earnest. "We regret what we did! We just wanted to mess around!"

"I know," Jake said, feeling a warmth in his heart. "But there's more to Christmas than just having fun. It's about kindness and sharing with others. If you two can truly understand this, I believe we can reverse the wish."

"What do we have to do?" Billy asked, his eyes wide with urgency.

The boys nodded, exchanging glances as they began to understand the gravity of their situation. "We want to come back, Jake! We want to help!" Billy cried out, his voice filled with sincerity.

"Then wish for that," Jake said, feeling hopeful. "Wish to come back and spread kindness instead of mischief." Tommy and Billy nodded vigorously, their faces now serious. "We wish to be back and to help others!" They shouted in unison, their voices echoing inside the globe.

The snow globe began to shimmer and shake once more, the swirling snow inside becoming a dazzling whirlwind of light. Jake took a step back, holding his breath as the energy pulsed and flared. He could feel the weight of their desire, the sincerity behind their words. In a ash of brilliant light, the snow globe exploded in a shower of sparkles, and for a moment, everything went quiet. Jake squinted against the brightness, shielding his eyes. When he opened them again, he saw Tommy and Billy standing in front of him, looking bewildered but free. "Jake!" they shouted, rushing toward him. "We're back!"

Jake embraced them in a hug, relief flooding through him. "You did it! I knew you could!" He exclaimed, feeling a wave of joy wash over him.

"We're so sorry for everything," Tommy said, his voice filled with sincerity. "We didn't understand how our actions affected you or anyone else. We just wanted to have fun."

Billy nodded, eyes wide with remorse. "We really do want to help. What can we do?"

Jake smiled, a warmth spreading in his chest. "Well, it is Christmas Eve. How about we help deliver these last few packages together? We can spread some holiday cheer instead of mischief."

The boys exchanged excited looks. "Yes! Let's do it!" they shouted, their spirits lifted.

Together, they hopped into the truck, and as they drove through the neighborhood, Jake felt a sense of fulfillment. The twins were different now, eager to make amends and share in the joy of giving. They laughed and cheered as they delivered gifts, helping neighbors carry packages, and even singing carols along the way.

As they finished their last delivery, the stars twinkled brightly overhead, and Jake realized that sometimes, the most magical moments come from understanding and kindness. The snow globe had taught them a valuable lesson, and in that spirit, they had forged a new bond.

When they returned to the truck, Jake looked at the boys and said, "Thank you for being willing to change. This Christmas will be one we won't forget."

And as the three of them sat in the warm glow of the truck's interior, Jake knew that they had all learned the true meaning of the season: that joy comes not from having everything, but from sharing what you have with others.

TWISTED CHRISTMAS

It was Christmas Eve, and the air was filled with the aroma of pine and Christmas cheer. In the small, snow-blanketed town of Maplewood, the spirit of the season typically brought joy to all. But for Steve, the holidays had taken a dark turn.

His wife, Laura, had been acting distant for weeks. Tonight, she told him she was going out with her mother, who pulled up in front of their modest home to pick her up. Steve pretended to be uninterested, but inside, a gnawing suspicion stirred. Something felt off.

As Laura climbed into the passenger seat of her mother's car, Steve's heart raced. Instead of waiting for her to return, he decided to follow them. He drove through the winding roads of Maplewood, his mind clouded with confusion and anger. Where could they be going?

The first stop was Laura's mother's house. They both exited her mother's car in the driveway and disappeared into the residence. About a half hour later, an unknown truck pulled up in front of the house, the engine kept running but the driver had killed the headlights. Steve was parked a ways back in front of a neighbor's house. It was hard to see anything. It looked like a person inside the truck was on their phone, like the light from a phone shining in the dark.

A few minutes later Laura came out the front door of the house and approached this truck. She opened the passenger door and climbed inside. The headlights came back on and the truck took off at a high speed. Steve tried to keep up with the truck but ended up loosing his tail. He continued down the dark road until he reached the next town. He slowed his vehicle's speed down to a crawl. He checked all the business parking lots and storefronts with his eyes, for her, for the truck. His hands were shaking and his blood pressure was running high.

Towards the end of town, just past Main Street, he spotted her, his wife, standing outside the stranger's truck. The truck was parked in the dirt lot of business of "Grumpy Uncle's Bar and Grill."

And then he saw him: a tall, athletic man with sandy hair. He parked across the street and watched. He watched as they laughed together, leaning in closer, their bodies entwined as they shared a passionate kiss.

Rage surged through Steve. He couldn't believe what he was witnessing. This was the man who had taken his wife away from him, the man who had broken their vows. In that moment, the Christmas spirit vanished, replaced by a chilling resolve.

With adrenaline coursing through his veins, he stepped out of the shadows, confronting them. "What the hell do you think you're doing?"

The couple froze, panic flickering in their eyes. Laura's mouth opened in disbelief as she realized who had interrupted their moment. "Steve! I—"

Before she could finish, Steve lunged at the new boyfriend, fists flying. The confrontation escalated quickly, turning into a violent struggle. With a surge of desperation, Steve pulled out a knife, one he had always kept in his front pocket for emergencies. The reflection of the cold blade glinted under the moonlight as he made a horrific decision.

Minutes later, he stood over the lifeless body of the man who had taken everything from him. Breathing heavily, he turned to Laura, who was watching in stunned silence.

"Well, what do you think?" Steve said, a manic grin spreading across his face. "Best Christmas present ever, right?"

Laura's eyes widened. A smile broke through her shock. "Steve! I was so worried you wouldn't like it! What took you so long to find me this time?"

They both felt a strange sense of unity in that moment. She walked toward him, wrapping her arms around his neck as if they were celebrating a victory.

Hand in hand, they returned to their car across the street, the world around them blanketed in snow, serene and untouched. The dead man lie still in the dirt.

"He never saw this coming, did he?" Steve said laughing hysterically.

They drove home together, a chilling bond forged in darkness.

As they entered their home, the Christmas decorations twinkled cheerfully, oblivious to the horror that had transpired. "Hot chocolate my dear?" Steve asked as he entered the kitchen.

"That sounds wonderful."

"Want to work out the plans, the details for next Christmas Eve?" Steve asked as he warmed the milk on the stove. He poured the hot milk into two mugs, one labeled, *I'm His* and the other labeled, *I'm Hers*. He poured in the chocolate powder and stirred each mug with a spoon.

"Yes, fantastic. I have some great ideas floating around in my head and can't wait to share them with you!"

WHO NEEDS SNOWFLAKES?

WHO NEEDS SNOWFLAKES WHEN YOU HAVE A GRANDPA?

When Christmas time comes around every year I always think of my grandpa. I always remember the last time I saw him alive. The last time I spoke to him. It was on a Christmas Eve fifteen years ago. I remember every moment I ever spent with him. Especially the moments from that evening. I can never forget them. That was the night he tried to tell everyone his secret. No one believed him, not even me. He had been a practical joker, and he made up the craziest stories to tell us all while we were gathered together in the same house during the holidays. Christmas time was time at the grandparent's house.

I never knew how my grandparents came to buy one of the biggest homes in Montana tucked away in the mountains. They had their very own lake. They eventually sold most of their acreage to allow others to build lake homes nearby. They were responsible for the town's success as well. They were super smart when it came to finances. Mathematical wizards. The town they pretty much created was called, Winter. Obviously named because it was cold as hell during the winter months and not much warmer in the summer months.

They had money. They made great investments. Everyone in town loved them. The neighbors around the lake adored them, respected them. Everyone that lived on the lake helped each other out without hesitation. It was the most perfect place in the world. Every Christmas my parents took my sister, my brother and I there to visit for two weeks leading up to Christmas Day. We had so much fun, swimming, fishing, boating, playing games together in the yard. At night we'd all sit around the fireplace playing board games and cards. I always thought my grandpa must've been some kind of big wig business man. Turns out I was no where close. My grandma had been a school teacher for over thirty years, I knew that. That's pretty much all I knew about them, other than the fact that they were the nicest, kindest, funniest people in the world!

I guess I'm ready now, ready to share the story. The story of the last Christmas Eve I ever shared with my grandpa.

-2-

We all spent the day down by the lake swimming. My dad, my brother, my nephews, and both my uncles and I played a game of tag football. I was having a blast. The sun went down early so I remember my mom rounding us kids up and telling everyone that dinner would be ready soon, that we needed to get inside soon and cleaned up, ready for supper!

We ate a great Christmas Eve meal and I knew right away I had eaten way too much food. My stomach was gargling and making weird noises. I knew a trip to the bathroom would be coming very soon. There was clanking in the kitchen as the women in our family began washing, drying, and putting away dishes and silverware. The coffee pot was brewing and the mugs had been handed out. Grandma was preparing hot chocolate for everyone who didn't want coffee. I couldn't wait! My Grandma gave me extra marshmallows in my mug. Everyone was back in the house and had changed into their Christmas pajamas and ugly sweaters. Board games were being brought into the living room and also being set up on the dining room table.

All of a sudden, Grandpa came in from the back porch. He had his cell phone in his hand. I wondered if he had gotten some kind of a phone call that had brought about his story he was about to tell us all.

Grandpa made an announcement telling everyone to please gather in the dining room area. I was lucky to get a seat at the table right beside him. The seats filled up and those who didn't get to sit stood by the table waiting to hear what Grandpa was about to tell us.

When everyone was present and eagerly waiting Grandpa began he cleared his throat. "I'm going to share something with all of you now, you may not believe me, I hope you do, but its okay if you don't. I've had a secret to tell for a very long time now." This is how he began to tell us his big secret. The one none of us believed, even me, remember?

"At an early age I joined the military, I believe you are all aware of this, it isn't any news, I know. But I left the military and became a secret agent. The kind that does things he isn't always proud to talk about, or couldn't ever talk about in my case. I've traveled the world, I don't thing there's a country out there I haven't set foot on. I'm telling you this now in case something were to happen to me."

"Dad, come on now! The kids don't know if you're serious or not." My mom spoke up from the other end of the table. She obviously didn't believe him already.

"I was. It is the truth. You all should know. No matter what I am always the man you have come to know, that part is real. My love for each and everyone of you is real. But I have been involved in some very sketchy things over the years and I've always been afraid that one day they might catch up to me. So I've said it. Not even Grandma knows so don't try to hit her up with a bunch of questions she can't answer. If you have questions, come and ask me directly. I'm now and open book. I feel a lot better now that you all know the truth. Thank you all so much for coming once again to our humble abode and sharing in this special time of the year. Now, let the games begin." And with that Grandpa was done with his story. He didn't go into any further details. He left it up to each and everyone of us to come to him with any questions we may had.

The room stood silent for two of the longest minutes. For me as a kid it seemed like thirty years passing by. Everyone quietly dispersed without comment heading to their chosen games to play. I had questions though.

Grandma and my mom came over and gave Grandpa a big hug. I joined in. I then watched Grandpa take his cup of coffee from Grandma and head out the back door out on to the porch. The sun was going down, the daylight was fading fast. Someone turned the Christmas music on and everyone was joining in singing Christmas songs together. I felt bad for my Grandpa. I wanted to talk to him, I had some questions, I didn't know that I believed him, that it was remotely possible that my grand father had been a secret government agent for most of his life. I wanted to believe him though, especially because it seemed like no one else did.

I grabbed a mug of hot chocolate and headed out the back door in pursuit of Grandpa. I didn't even care that Grandma hadn't had the chance to slip in extra marshmallows for me.

Grandpa had made his way down to the lake, he was watching the sunset on the boat dock. He stood, mug in one hand, his other hand in his pocket.

He appeared to be lost in deep thought when I approached him on the dock. What could Grandpa be thinking about?

"Grandpa?" I called out, my voice breaking the tranquil silence.

Grandpa turned around slowly, a smile breaking through his contemplative expression. "Hey there, sport. What are you doing out here?"

I hesitated, fidgeting with the sleeve of my sweater. "I was just wondering... are you really a secret agent?"

Grandpa chuckled softly, kneeling down to meet me at eye level. "Well, that's a story for you to decide. I was completely honest in there, Riley. Let me tell you something more important, it doesn't matter what I did before. What matters is the time we spend together now."

"Was it cool? Did you fight bad guys?" I was nervous for some reason when I asked.

Grandpa's smile faded slightly, replaced by a glimmer of something deeper. "It was a different world, Riley.

Not all adventures are as glamorous as they seem. Sometimes, the hardest battles are the ones we fight to protect the people we love."

I gave him a nod even thought I didn't quite understand his words of wisdom at the time. "So, you were brave?"

"Bravery comes in many forms," Grandpa replied, glancing at the lake. "Sometimes it's about standing up for what's right, and other times it's simply being there for your family."

"Like when you always come to my soccer games?"

"Exactly," Grandpa said, ruing my hair. "I might not wear a tuxedo or have gadgets like James Bond, but I'm still your grandpa, and I'll always be your biggest fan."

As we stood together, the sun began to dip below the horizon, painting the sky with vibrant oranges and purples. I looked back at the house, where laughter and warmth was spilling out from inside, and I realized something.

"Can I be brave too?" I asked him, in my small voice.

"Absolutely," Grandpa replied, placing a reassuring hand on my shoulder. "Bravery isn't about being fearless; it's about facing your fears and doing what's right. You already show it every day, just by being you. I love you a bunch kiddo."

"Grandpa?"

"Yes young man?" I always loved how patient he had been with me.

"I believe your story."

He smiled. This man was my hero, I realized it at that very moment in time. I wanted to be just like him when I grew up. I didn't want to press him with anymore questions, even though I had plenty, plenty more to ask.

I left him on the boat dock and headed back inside to join my siblings in a game of Monopoly, one of my favorites even though I was always the first player out every time. When I climbed up the steps to the porch I turned to my Grandpa for one more look. That's when my world really changed forever.

I froze in place. All I could do is watch from far away on the porch as they came and took my Grandpa away. I ran inside afterwards and fell straight into my mother's arms.

-2-

"You're never gonna believe me, Mom!" I took her by the hand and pulled her towards the backdoor and then out onto the back porch.

"What do you mean, sweetheart?" Mom whispered to me brushing a stray hair from my forehead. She glanced toward the lake, but all she saw was the rippling water and the faint outline of the distant shore.

"Grandpa! He was a secret agent! I swear! They just took him!" My voice trembled with excitement and fear.

"Riley, what are you talking about?" Mom frowned, trying to make sense of my words. "What do you mean, a secret agent? He was just telling us stories at dinner."

"No, Mom, I mean it! He told us he had a secret. I thought it was just a joke too, but it's real!" I pointed toward the lake, where the boats had vanished. "They had masks and everything! It was like a movie!"

A mix of concern and skepticism was no doubt swirling in her mind, "Riley, you're just imagining things. Grandpa was playing around, right? He was just being silly."

I shook my head vigorously. "No! I'm serious! I saw them grab him! They put a bag over his head! He didn't even fight back!"

Just then, the rest of the family began to gather, drawn by the commotion. Grandma, with her silver hair and kind smile, looked at me with worry. "What's wrong, dear?"

"Grandpa's gone! They took him!" I cried.

"Who took him?" Grandma asked, her eyes narrowing as she tried to piece together what was happening.

"Some guys in speedboats! They looked like soldiers! They took him!"

The laughter and warmth of the Christmas gathering was instantly replaced by a cold, uneasy tension. My Mom exchanged glances with my Dad, who shrugged in confusion. "This doesn't make any sense," he muttered.

Yes, there was an investigation. It went on for nearly a year. The police and neighbors searched every square inch of the lake and the properties around the lake. In a nutshell, no evidence of a crime was ever discovered.

I promised myself on Christmas night that I would make myself forget what I had seen. No one really believed me anyway. I told the truth, just like my Grandpa had.

I never forgot what really happened, only pushed it into a locked cabinet in the back of my memories. I replaced it with a fake one that goes like this:

As the Christmas Eve evening fell and the stars began to twinkle above, Grandpa and I headed back inside after our talk, after I told him I believed his story, hand in hand, ready to join the rest of the family. In that moment, the secret of Grandpa's past faded away, replaced by the warmth of togetherness and the promise of new adventures yet to come.

THE VISITOR

The snow fell softly outside Clara's quaint little home, blanketing the world in a hush that only Christmas Eve could bring. Inside, the warmth of the flickering re danced across the walls, and the scent of pine from the small tree in the corner mingled with the rich aroma of freshly baked cookies. Yet, despite the festive atmosphere, Clara felt an emptiness that echoed through the silence.

After losing her husband, Henry, two years prior, Christmas had transformed from a season of joy into a painful reminder of her loneliness. She had once reveled in the magic of the holiday, but now, it felt like a ghost of what it had been, a time filled with laughter now replaced by a heavy stillness.

As she sat wrapped in her favorite blanket, sipping her tea and watching the flames flicker, a sudden knock at the door startled her. She hadn't expected any visitors, especially not on a night like this. Hesitating for a moment, she rose from her chair and opened the door.

Standing on her doorstep was a man, his silhouette framed by the glow of the porch light. He wore an old brown overcoat, a wool scarf wrapped snugly around his neck, and a hat pulled low over his brow. Clara squinted, trying to decipher this unexpected guest's face, but the shadows hid his features.

"Good evening, ma'am," he said, his voice warm and familiar, sending a chill down her spine. "May I come in? It's frightfully cold out here."

Clara hesitated, but something in his voice tugged at her heart. "Of course," she replied, stepping aside. "Please, make yourself comfortable."

As he entered, the man removed his hat, and Clara inhaled sharply. She recognized him immediately. The sharp blue eyes and the gentle smile were unmistakable, this was Henry. But how could it be? He had been gone for two years.

"Clara," he said softly, and she felt her heart ache at the sound of her name on his lips. "It's good to see you again."

"Is this real?" she stammered, her voice trembling. "Are you really here?"

"In a way," he replied, his tone laced with a bittersweet love for her. "I've come to share something important with you."

She led him to the living room, her hands shaking as she poured him a cup of tea. The warmth of the re illuminated his features, and for a moment, she lost herself in the memory of their life together. The laughter, the love, and the bittersweet moments that had defined their years.

"Why now?" she finally asked, her voice barely above a whisper. "Why on Christmas Eve?"

"Because it's a time for reflection," he said, taking a sip of his tea. "A time when the veil between worlds is at its thinnest. I wanted to help you find peace, Clara. You've been holding onto so much pain."

As the clock struck midnight, the room shifted, and Clara felt a weight descend upon her. Memories flooded back, unspoken words, arguments left unresolved, and secrets buried deep within her heart. "I've missed you so much," she confessed, tears streaming down her cheeks. "But I never told you how I truly felt. I was angry... angry that you left me alone."

Henry's expression softened. "I know, love. And I'm sorry for the hurt you've carried. But it's time to let go. You've kept your heart locked away, and it's time to open it again."

"What do you mean?" Clara asked, her voice trembling.

"It's not just about letting go of me," he said, his eyes piercing through her. "It's about letting go of the past. You've hidden from life, from joy. You need to face the ghosts that haunt you, the regrets, the fears."

With each word, Clara felt the heaviness in her heart begin to lift. She saw the shadows of her past swirl around her, their forms shifting and changing as they danced in the relight. There were moments of happiness she had forgotten, laughter shared with friends, and family gatherings filled with love.

"I'm ready," she whispered, her heart swelling with a newfound courage. "I want to live again."

Henry smiled, and the warmth of his presence enveloped her. "That's all I needed to hear. Remember, love is never truly lost. It stays with you, guiding you even when you can't see it."

As the clock chimed one, Clara felt a gentle breeze fill the room, and the shadows began to fade. Henry reached out, brushing his fingers against her cheek, a final caress that spoke of love eternal. "Merry Christmas, Clara."

And just like that, he was gone, leaving behind the warmth of his spirit and the promise of a new beginning. Clara sat alone in the quiet room, but the silence no longer felt heavy. The Christmas tree twinkled with lights, and outside, the snow continued to fall, sparkling like stars in the night.

With a deep breath, Clara rose from her chair, feeling lighter than she had in years. She walked to the window, gazing out at the winter wonderland, the Moon lighting up the sky, and for the first time in a long while, she smiled. The ghosts of her past had come to visit, but they had not come to stay. They had given her a gift, the chance to embrace the life that lay ahead, with hope, love, and the promise of new memories waiting to be made.

Clara poured another cup of tea. She carried it outside and sat on her porch, the tea cradled in her hands. It was late but she knew there was no way she'd be able to get a wink of sleep after seeing Henry again.

-2-

It had been two years since her husband, Thomas, had disappeared during a hiking trip in the nearby woods. She had been told he was presumed dead, but the ache in her heart held onto a fragile thread of hope that perhaps he was still out there, lost but alive. She sat looking o into the horizon, the sky painted in hues of orange and pink, a soft humming sound in the air, pulling Clara from her thoughts. She looked up, squinting at the sky, when a shimmering light descended, illuminating her porch like a spotlight. She gasped, her heart racing as a figure emerged from the brilliance. At first she thought it might be her love Henry coming back to her, to tell her he changed his mind, that he was coming back home. What she saw wasn't anything like Henry at all, not even close.

Instead of Henry, she saw a tall, slender being with skin that glimmered like starlight approaching her.

It was as if her world had been frozen momentarily and she was moving in slow motion.

"Clara," the being spoke, its voice a harmonious blend of tones that resonated deep within her. "I am Elara, a messenger from the Intergalactic Alliance."

Clara blinked in disbelief, her mind racing. "What do you want?" She asked.

"I brought you Henry," Elara said, tilting its head, eyes shimmering with a depth that seemed to hold galaxies. "He wanted to let you know he isn't dead. He is alive, but he is not been here on your world." Confusion washed over her. "What do you mean? Where has he been?" "Henry has been working with us," Elara explained, its form pulsating with light. "He volunteered to assist our efforts in studying your planet, its people, and its culture. We require his expertise, his creativity. He asked if I'd be the one to explain where he has been."

"Why didn't he come back?" Clara's voice trembled. "Why didn't he tell me?"

"He chose to protect you," Elara replied gently. "The work is dangerous, and revealing our existence would have put you in peril. But now, we have a proposal."

Clara's heart raced. "What kind of proposal?"

Elara took a step closer,"Henry will continue his work, but he wishes to know that you are safe and that you can move forward with your life. He needs your blessing."

Tears welled in Clara's eyes. She had longed for closure, yet the thought of Henry living among aliens was almost too surreal to comprehend. "If he's alive, if he's okay... I want him to be happy. If you can promise me this than..."

Elara nodded, "Then let him know it is alright to continue. You are free to live, to love again, and he will find peace in that knowledge."

With a deep breath, Clara closed her eyes, envisioning her husband, the way he laughed, the way he held her close. "Tell him I love him. I always will. He can keep doing what he needs to do."

A wave of warmth came over her, and when she opened her eyes, Elara was smiling. "Your bond is strong. He will feel your love, and it will guide him."

"Will I ever see him again?" she whispered, a part of her still holding onto hope.

"Perhaps," Elara said, its voice echoing like a distant star. "But for now, live your life, and know that he is safe."

With that, Elara vanished into the night sky, leaving Clara with a heart full of bittersweet emotion. She glanced at the stars above, feeling a connection to Henry that transcended the void of space and time. She realized that love, even when stretched across galaxies, could never truly die.

From that day on, Clara began to embrace life again, carrying Henry's memory with her while allowing herself the freedom to heal. In the quiet moments, she would look up at the stars, whispering her love into the cosmos, knowing that somewhere out there, Henry was listening.

UNDER THE MISTLETOE

Joey had always loved Christmas. The the twinkling lights, the Christmas music, the feeling in the air of joy, and the smell of pine filled his heart. This year, however, his holiday spirit was dampened by the unsettling atmosphere in his grandparents' old house. It was a creaky, charming place filled with family memorabilia and the scent of cinnamon. Yet, an unshakable feeling of dread hung in the air, like a thick fog.

Joey and his mother had moved in with her parents after the horrible divorce. His grand parents had built a large cabin out in the woods and up in the mountains years ago. They lived not far from town and were very well liked. Joey's grandfather had made a fortune all on his own. He had no idea how he just knew this was the best case scenario for him and his mom, a chance to restart their lives away from his crazy abusive father.

Joey's grandparents offered him a room of his own. The only catch was that this room was also the attic. Well insulated and lots of room for a young kid to enjoy.

As Joey helped his grandmother decorate the house for the holidays, he noticed a strange wooden box tucked away in the attic. Curiosity piqued, he climbed up the rickety stairs and opened it. Inside, he found a collection of old newspaper clippings, each detailing unsolved murders in nearby towns. Each article was dated around Christmas, with the same eerie detail: a sprig of mistletoe found near each victim.

Joey's heart raced as he read the headlines. "Local Woman Found Dead on Christmas Eve," "Mysterious Deaths Plague the Town," "Missing Persons Linked to Christmas Cheer." The last article was dated just a week ago, and the face of the victim looked hauntingly familiar. It was a girl from Joey's high school.

He clutched the box, suddenly feeling the weight of his discovery. He had to talk to someone, but who would believe him?

As he descended the stairs, he overheard his grandparents in the kitchen, their voices low and conspiratorial.

"Did you hear about the girl?" His grandfather said, a hint of excitement in his voice. "She was perfect. Just like the others."

Joey's heart sank. He pressed his ear against that separated the living room from the kitchen, listening intently.

"We have to be careful. We can't let anyone find out." His grandmother replied, and Joey felt a chill run down his spine. "It's tradition, after all. We do it for the family."

The pieces began fitting together, and Joey felt sick to his stomach. His grandparents weren't just eccentric; they were killers. The mistletoe was more than just a decoration, it was their calling card.

That night, as the snow fell gently outside, Joey decided he couldn't stay silent any longer. Armed with his phone, he covertly recorded their conversation as they reminisced about the past and their "traditions."

They had no idea he was hiding in the nearby bushes on the backside of the house. His grandparents were drinking coffee while they sat in their wooden back porch rockers.

He learned that every year, they picked someone from the community to eliminate, believing that each kill brought them closer to something greater, something that the family had protected for generations.

With his heart pounding, he set his alarm clock to go o at four o' clock in the morning. He had lifted his grandparents set of car keys from the key holder by the doorway. He would wake up and sneak out of the house, roll his grandparents car down the driveway, and then start it up so they wouldn't hear it. He would head into town and talk to the sheriff.

His mother had been sent by his grandparents on an all expenses paid girls only vacation with her friends somewhere in the Florida Keys. She wasn't due to return until the next week.

He woke up ten minutes before his alarm clock was set to go off. He dressed quickly, slowly opened his door to his room, and tiptoed down the staircase with his pair of shoes in one hand. He made his away across the living room to the front door. Once he opened the front door he ran at full speed towards the car in the driveway.

He set out on his way to the sheriff's office in town. He knew he had to act quickly. The sheriff's deputies listened intently, and with Joey's evidence, the recording of his grandparents discussing the murders, they launched an investigation. For two long weeks Joey waited for something to happen, for the sheriff's office to come knocking on the door. He was extremely happy his mother had come home. He hadn't summoned up the courage to tell her about his findings.

As Christmas approached, Joey felt the weight of the world on his shoulders.

On Christmas Eve, as the family gathered to celebrate, the atmosphere was thick with tension.

The doorbell rang just as Joey's grandmother brought out a tray of cookies, each adorned with a sprig of mistletoe. Joey exchanged a nervous glance with his grandfather, who smiled too widely.

Suddenly, the door burst open, and the police swarmed inside, catching his grandparents off guard. "You're under arrest for multiple counts of murder," one deputy declared, the words echoing in the small room.

In the ensuing chaos, Joey felt a strange mix of relief and sorrow. His grandparents were taken away, and as he watched them go, he couldn't shake the feeling that something dark and twisted had been lurking beneath the surface of his family all along.

As the holiday season came to a close, Joey sat in his room, staring at the now-empty attic. He had uncovered the truth, but at what cost? Christmas would never be the same. The once joyful holiday now carried the weight of the mistletoe murders, a chilling reminder of the darkness that could reside even in the most seemingly loving families.

He heard a knock at the door. "Come in!" He called out.

His mom opened the door and entered the room. "This attic brings back a lot of memories." She said as she crossed the floor towards Joey who was sitting on his bed with his back to the headboard.

"Mom. I'm so sorry for everything."

"Nothing to be sorry about Joey. It is what it is. Life throws you curve balls and if you're not ready for them well, you won't be able to hit the ball right?" Joey knew this was something she had probably picked up from his dad's baseball knowledge since he had been a big fan of the sport. She was just trying to set his mind at ease. He knew that she was depressed and unhappy. First the divorce, then this, her own parents serial killers? Where would they go from here? How could they even hope to move past this all?

"You're a great kid. I don't tell you enough. I love you so much."

"I love you too mom, please don't cry. It's going to be alright." His mom sat down beside him on his bed. He wrapped his arms around her and held her tightly.

She patted one of his arms, wiped the tears away from her eyes with her sweater sleeve. She stood up and walked to the doorway, then stopped.

Joey watched as she crossed the room. He wanted to speak comforting words to her, but he had none. She turned her head towards Joey, "We made some breakfast. A big breakfast. Eggs, pancakes, bacon, sausage, strawberries freshly picked from the backyard. Won't you come join us?"

"Oh, that sounds so good!" He shouted from across the room. Then it hit him. Did she say, Join US? Who is US? "Is there someone else joining us mom?"

"Yes. The sheriff is downstairs with your grandparents waiting for us to join them. Did you know the sheriff is your Grandfather's best friend? Yeah, they are hunting buddies, known each other their entire lives. I suggest you don't take long to get down there. It seems they have a lot to talk to you about. I guess I do too."

CHRISTMAS LIGHTS

The Johnson family prided themselves on their Christmas spirit. Every year, they transformed their suburban home into a dazzling wonderland of twinkling lights, inflatable snowmen, and a life-sized Santa on the roof. This year, however, they had outdone themselves, stringing up thousands of LED bulbs that sparkled like the stars in the winter sky.

As dusk fell on December 1st, the neighborhood gathered to witness the grand unveiling. Children squealed in delight, and parents snapped photos, but as the final switch was flipped, a strange energy crackled in the air. The brilliant lights pulsated, glowing brighter and then dimming, as if responding to an unseen force.

"Did you see that?" Whispered Lily, the youngest Johnson, clutching her mother's hand.

"Just a glitch, honey." Her mother, Olivia, reassured, though she couldn't shake the chill that crept up her spine.

That night, as the family settled in for hot cocoa and holiday movies, the lights began to flicker ominously. The room darkened and brightened in an unsettling rhythm, creating eerie shadows that danced across the walls. "It's just a power surge," Noah, Lily's father, said with forced calm, but deep down, he felt a stirring unease.

The next evening, Lily noticed something odd. The air outside felt thick, heavy with anticipation. As she pressed her nose against the window, she saw the lights flicker in a pattern, one that resembled a heartbeat. Heart racing, she turned to her family, "I think the lights are trying to tell us something."

"Lights can't talk, sweetie," Noah chuckled, but his smile faltered when he caught a glimpse of the flickering display. It seemed to pulse with a life of its own, and shadows twisted unnaturally in the yard.

Days passed, and the lights grew more erratic. Neighbors reported strange occurrences: pets acting strangely, whispers in the wind, and a lingering darkness that crept into their homes. The Johnsons' house, once a beacon of holiday cheer, became the epicenter of the growing unease.

One night, Olivia woke to a soft, haunting melody drifting through the air. It was as though the lights were singing, a lullaby that beckoned her to the window. She hesitated, but curiosity pulled her closer. As she peered out, she gasped at the sight. The lights were no longer just decorations; they shimmered with an otherworldly glow, forming shapes that twisted and curled like smoke.

"Mom?" Lily's voice trembled from the hallway. "I don't like the lights anymore."

Olivia turned, feeling a cold dread settle in her stomach. "Let's go to bed, sweetie. Everything is fine."

But everything was not fine. That night, the flickering escalated into a chaotic frenzy. The Johnsons huddled together in the living room, surrounded by the pulsing glow. "We need to turn them o," Noah said, his voice steady despite the fear in his eyes.

As they raced outside, the lights flickered violently, as if protesting their decision. Shadows swirled around them. "Hurry!" Olivia cried, scrambling to the control box.

With shaking hands, she flipped the switch, but the lights continued to blaze. The melody grew louder, more insistent, drowning out their cries. "It's not just the lights!" Lily screamed, pointing at the shadows enveloping their home. "It's something else!"

In that moment, Noah recalled the old stories the neighborhood kids shared around bonfires when he was younger. Tales of a dark spirit that fed on joy, awakening only when the lights shined too bright.

"We've unleashed it!" He shouted, realizing their festive display had turned into a beacon for the malevolent force.

Together, in the middle of the front yard, they held each other's hands forming a circle. They closed their eyes and concentrated on the warmth of their love, the joy of their memories. The flickering lights dimmed, and the shadows hesitated, drawn to the bright energy of their bond.

With a final, desperate push, they shouted, "We choose love, not darkness!" The air crackled, and a brilliant white light exploded from their circle, washing over the yard like a tidal wave.

The shadows shrieked and recoiled, dissipating into the night. The lights blinked one final time before settling into a soft, steady glow. Exhausted but relieved, the family collapsed on the lawn, their hearts racing.

As dawn broke, the neighborhood awoke to find the Johnson home aglow with a warm, inviting light. The malevolent force had been banished, leaving behind only the spirit of Christmas. They had extinguished the darkness, but the experience lingered like a whisper in the air, a reminder that even the brightest lights can attract shadows.

CUL-DE-SAC THIEF

In the quiet cul-de-sac of Maple Lane, Christmas had arrived with its usual charm. Lights twinkled on every house. That wonderful feeling of Christmas time was in the air once again. But this year, an unexpected mystery had cast a shadow over the festive spirit. One by one, the neighbors' Christmas trees began to vanish from their yards. Someone had gone out late at night and had stolen all the trees! Whispers of a Christmas thief spread like wildfire.

The neighbors on Maple Lane celebrated each Christmas by getting a bunch of Christmas trees delivered to the cul-de-sac. They would help each other each bring a tree to their front yard. Each family household would then decorate their Christmas tree in their yard. Neighbors from the next street down would then all arrive in their golf carts and one by one score and judge each Christmas tree on Maple Lane to determine the winner! It was a fun, entertaining, and exciting way for the the two neighborhoods to come together at Christmas time and intermingle with one another.

Twelve-year-old Max, who lived with his mom at 1842 Maple Lane was determined to uncover the truth about the Christmas tree thefts. His mother, Charlotte, a spirited woman with a knack for solving puzzles, and a published children's mystery author sensed her son's excitement and decided to join him in his sleuthing adventure.

Together, they turned their living room into a command center, complete with a whiteboard filled with suspects and clues.

"Okay, Max," Charlotte said, pointing to the board. "We need to figure out who had the opportunity to steal the trees. Who do we know that was out late at night?"

Max scratched his head. "Well, there's Mr. Jenkins. He always walks his dog around midnight. And Mrs. Thompson has been acting a little strange since her husband passed. She loves Christmas, but this year, she's been distant."

"Good observations," Charlotte replied, jotting down their names. "Let's start by talking to them."

Their first stop was Mr. Jenkins. As they approached his porch, they saw him sitting in his rocking chair, a steaming mug of cocoa in hand.

"Evening, Mr. Jenkins!" Max called out, trying to sound casual. "Have you noticed anything odd around the neighborhood lately?"

Mr. Jenkins chuckled, his eyes twinkling behind his glasses. "Odd? Just the usual ruckus, I suppose. But I did hear some rustling by Mrs. Thompson's house last night. Might want to check there."

Max exchanged a glance with his mother. "Thanks, Mr. Jenkins!"

Next, they headed over to Mrs. Thompson's house, where they found her peering through her window, a frown on her face.

"Hello, Mrs. Thompson," Charlotte said warmly. "We were just wondering if you'd seen anything suspicious lately?"

Mrs. Thompson sighed, her eyes glistening. "I've been too wrapped up in my own thoughts. But I did hear a loud thump around nine o' clock last night. It sounded like it came from the woods. I guess it could've been the sound of someone dragging a tree? Those trees are special to the neighborhood. My son and I are majorly upset that someone would do such a thing! We were all ready to start decorating tonight! We planned on winning this year!"

Max felt a surge of excitement. "Can we check it out, Mom?"

"Absolutely," Charlotte replied, feeling the thrill of the chase.

As they ventured into the nearby woods behind Mrs. Thompson's house the chilly air nipped at their cheeks. They followed the trail back deep into the woods. They stumbled upon a clearing, where they were startled to find a cluster of Christmas trees, each adorned with lights and ornaments, as if someone had thrown a secret holiday party.

"Look!" Max exclaimed, pointing. "Those are the stolen trees!"

Suddenly, they heard giggles. Hiding behind a tree were three of Max's friends, Keith, Heather, and Sam, all with guilty expressions.

"Surprise!" Keith said sheepishly. When the three saw that Max's mother, an adult was with him, Keith added, "We didn't want to ruin Christmas, but we thought it would be fun to borrow the trees to have a secret party."

Max's face fell. "You guys scared us! We thought there was a thief!"

"We're sorry!" Heather chimed in. "We were just trying to make Christmas a little more fun. We'll return them right away."

Charlotte smiled, relieved but rm. "You need to apologize to your neighbors and help them put their trees back. Christmas is about sharing and being together, not sneaking around."

As the group returned to the cul-de-sac, carrying the trees back, one by one, the neighbors had begun gathering in the cul-de-sac with confusion written all over their faces. But their frowns quickly turned into laughter as the kids admitted to what they had done, and explained their intentions.

That evening, the cul-de-sac was filled with a renewed sense of community. Everyone pitched in to decorate the trees together, transforming the night into an unexpected celebration. Max and his mother exchanged proud smiles, knowing that their little adventure had not only solved the mystery but had also brought their neighborhood closer together.

As they headed home, Max turned to his mother. "Thanks for teaming up with me, Mom. This was the best Christmas mystery ever!"

Charlotte chuckled, wrapping her arm around him. "Anytime, partner. Next year, let's just stick to decorating cookies."

And with that, they walked home, hearts warm with the spirit of the season, ready to embrace whatever the next adventure might bring.

www.ingramcontent.com/pod-product-compliance
Lightning Source LLC
Chambersburg PA
CBHW020511160726
47991CB00007B/2900

CENTER OF PEDAGOGY

Junior Faculty Progress Report
Early Childhood and Elementary Education

Student's Name _Marisa Landis_   Date 4/7/09   Visit # 5
School _______________   Subject/Grade level 3
Your Name _______________
Your Position: ☑ Education Mentor   ☐ Cooperating Teacher   _Formal_

Does not meet expectations	Meets expectations	Exceeds expectations
(1) (2)	(3) (4)	(5)

Please circle the appropriate rating for each criterion listed below **using the accompanying RUBRIC**.

1. **PLANNING FOR STUDENT LEARNING**
   a. Stating clear, meaningful, and dev. appropriate learning goals/objectives: 1 2 3 4 **(5)**
   b. Organizing subject matter for student learning: 1 2 3 4 **(5)**
   c. Creative and dev. appropriate learning activities and materials: 1 2 3 4 **(5)**
   d. Adaptations based on obs. & assessment of children's strengths and needs: 1 2 3 4 **(5)**
   e. Content related to children's interests and communities: 1 2 3 4 **(5)**

   This Social Studies lesson was well planned and organized.

2. **TEACHING FOR STUDENT LEARNING**
   a. Making content in each discipline comprehensible to students: 1 2 3 4 **(5)**
   b. Monitoring understanding, providing feedback, and adapting activities   1 2 3 4 **(5)**
   c. Using media and other technology in appropriate ways: 1 2 3 4 **(5)**
   d. Promoting critical thinking: 1 2 3 4 **(5)**
   e. Using democratic practices: respect for child's culture and language   1 2 3 4 **(5)**
   f. Using range of teaching strategies based on understanding of child dev: 1 2 3 4 **(5)**
   g. Making curriculum meaningful to all children: 1 2 3 4 **(5)**

   The students were engaged in learning.

3. **ASSESSING STUDENT LEARNING**
   a. Recording and using assessment results to inform instruction: 1 2 3 4 **(5)**
   b. Using a range of assessment tools to document student strengths: 1 2 3 4 **(5)**

4. **CREATING A POSITIVE ENVIRONMENT FOR STUDENT LEARNING**
   a. Establishing a classroom community that fosters respectful behaviors: 1 2 3 4 **(5)**
   b. Providing a safe physical environment conducive to learning: 1 2 3 4 **(5)**
   c. Using instructional time effectively: 1 2 3 4 **(5)**
   d. Creating responsive and caring relationships with children and adults: 1 2 3 4 **(5)**

5. **PROFESSIONALISM**
   a. Expressing ideas clearly and personal attributes: 1 2 3 4 **(5)**
   b. Communicating with others to support student learning: 1 2 3 4 **(5)**
   c. Reflecting on instructional efforts: 1 2 3 4 **(5)**

Please write additional comments below or attach them to this page.

Marisa is creative and highly involved in developing her teaching skills. She is a natural teacher.

Signature: _______________

CENTER OF PEDAGOGY

Junior Faculty Progress Report

Early Childhood and Elementary Education

Student's Name *Marisa Landy*   Date 3/24/09 Visit # 4

School ▮▮▮▮▮▮▮▮▮▮▮▮▮▮▮▮   Subject/Grade level 3

Your Name ▮▮▮▮▮▮▮▮▮▮

Your Position: ☑ Education Mentor   ☐ Cooperating Teacher

Does not meet expectations	Meets expectations	Exceeds expectations
(1) (2)	(3) (4)	(5)

Please circle the appropriate rating for each criterion listed below <u>using the accompanying RUBRIC</u>.

1. **PLANNING FOR STUDENT LEARNING**
   a. Stating clear, meaningful, and dev. appropriate learning goals/objectives: 1 2 3 4 **(5)**
   b. Organizing subject matter for student learning: 1 2 3 4 **(5)**
   c. Creative and dev. appropriate learning activities and materials: 1 2 3 4 **(5)**
   d. Adaptations based on obs. & assessment of children's strengths and needs: 1 2 3 4 **(5)**
   e. Content related to children's interests and communities: 1 2 3 4 **(5)**

2. **TEACHING FOR STUDENT LEARNING**
   a. Making content in each discipline comprehensible to students: 1 2 3 4 **(5)**
   b. Monitoring understanding, providing feedback, and adapting activities 1 2 3 4 **(5)**
   c. Using media and other technology in appropriate ways: 1 2 3 4 **(5)**
   d. Promoting critical thinking: 1 2 3 4 **(5)**
   e. Using democratic practices: respect for child's culture and language 1 2 3 4 **(5)**
   f. Using range of teaching strategies based on understanding of child dev: 1 2 3 4 **(5)**
   g. Making curriculum meaningful to all children: 1 2 3 4 **(5)**

3. **ASSESSING STUDENT LEARNING**
   a. Recording and using assessment results to inform instruction: 1 2 3 4 **(5)**
   b. Using a range of assessment tools to document student strengths: 1 2 3 4 **(5)**

4. **CREATING A POSITIVE ENVIRONMENT FOR STUDENT LEARNING**
   a. Establishing a classroom community that fosters respectful behaviors: 1 2 3 4 **(5)**
   b. Providing a safe physical environment conducive to learning: 1 2 3 4 **(5)**
   c. Using instructional time effectively: 1 2 3 4 **(5)**
   d. Creating responsive and caring relationships with children and adults: 1 2 3 4 **(5)**

5. **PROFESSIONALISM**
   a. Expressing ideas clearly and personal attributes: 1 2 3 4 **(5)**
   b. Communicating with others to support student learning: 1 2 3 4 **(5)**
   c. Reflecting on instructional efforts: 1 2 3 4 **(5)**

Please write additional comments below or attach them to this page.

Marisa has fine qualities to establish herself as a future teacher. She is creative, energetic and highly intrested in developing and fine tuning her teaching skills.

"Diary of a…" Writing with Perspective

Lesson Rationale and Context: I am teaching this lesson in order to encourage students to use ideas from books they love, in order to inspire creative writing of their own. The book *Diary of a Worm*, by Doreen Cronin, is all about the perspective of another creature. I think this book offers a great opportunity for young readers and writers to think outside of the box. This also allows for readers to integrate fiction and non-fiction texts into one activity. Students will be working with partners to learn about different creatures through a non-fiction text and write a diary from their perspective.

Goal: Each student will listen to the read aloud, *Diary of a Worm*. Then, they will work with a partner to read a non-fiction book about an animal or insect and write a diary of that creature using facts located in the non-fiction books.

Essential Question: What is perspective and how can it be used in writing?

Objectives: Student will be able to:

1. Understand perspective and apply the concept of perspective to their writing.
2. Read and understand a non-fiction book.
3. Use a graphic organizer to help plan for writing.
4. Write a diary entry from their creature's perspective.

NJCCCS:

Standard 3.1.2 (Reading) All students will understand and apply the knowledge of sounds, letters, and words in written English to become independent and fluent readers and will read a variety of materials and texts with fluency and comprehension.

> G. Comprehension Skills and Response to Text
>> 1. Demonstrate ability to recall facts and details of text.
>
> H. Inquiry and Research
>> 2. Read a variety of non-fiction and fiction books and produce evidence of reading.

Standard 3.2.2 (Writing) All students will write in clear, concise, organized language that varies in content and form for different audiences and purposes.

> A. Writing as a Process (prewriting, drafting, revising, editing, postwriting)
>> 1. Generate ideas for writing. hearing stories, recalling experiences, brainstorming, and drawing.
>> 6. Use graphic organizers to assist with planning writing.

Materials:

- *Diary of a Worm* by Doreen Cronin
- Non-fiction books:
- *Where Do Chicks Come From?* By Amy E. Sklansky, *From Tadpole to Frog* by Wendy Pfeffer,, *What's It Like to Be a Fish* by Wendy Pfeffer, and *From Caterpillar to Butterfly* by Deborah Heiligman
- "Diary of a…" booklet, "Diary of a…" graphic organizer, Diary of a Fly Chart Paper Journal Entry, Graphic Organizer Poster, post-its, pencils, fly swatter, pool skimmer, giant hand

Anticipatory Set:

I will tell the children that we will be doing a writing activity today. Sometimes authors use ideas from other authors. We will read *Diary of a Worm*, to inspire us to write a diary of another creature. I will explain to them that this book is all about the "perspective" of a worm. I will ask if anyone thinks they know what "perspective" means. As we read, I will ask the children to try to figure out what "perspective" means. Next, I will read *Diary of a Worm*, by Doreen Cronin, aloud to the class. I will ask the children what they think perspective means. I will guide them with questions as needed. I will explain to the children that perspective is the way you see things. Now, I will take out a fly swatter and ask if anyone knows what this is used for. I will show them what I would look like if I swatted a fly. I will tell them to close their eyes. When they open their eyes, they will have the perspective of a fly. I will have a giant hand and a pool skimmer as my fly swatter. Now, I can ask them how a fly will feel. What is perspective?

Lesson Procedure:

1. Modeling-
    a. I will introduce the group activity to the children. I will tell them that they will be working with a partner to understand the perspective of another creature.
    b. When thinking about the fly, we will use the **poster size graphic organizer** to help guide our thought. This includes the following questions: What would I learn in school? What would my nightmares be about? Who would I be friends with? What would kids say if they saw me?
    c. I will ask them to help me write about the fly scenario. I have **journal chart paper** that I can use to write a journal entry of the fly. I will start the first sentence by writing, "June 23rd – Today I had to fly for my life!"
2. Joint Participation
    a. I will ask the children to help me finish the journal entry. They can add something like, "A giant tried to squash me! I flew left and I flew right! I made it out just in time! Shhhh! Don't tell mom that I came that close to a human!"
3. Guided Practice
    a. The children will work together to read the **non-fiction books** provided on their creature. I put post-its on the pages that I feel they should definitely read. I will explain to them that sometimes when you are looking for facts and reading non-fiction you don't have to read the whole book to find what you need.
    b. They will also use the **graphic organizer** to keep track of their facts and ideas.
4. Independent Work
    a. Now that the children know more about their creature, they are ready to write their journal entries from their perspective. They each have an introduction to their creature in their booklet. They will work to write journal entries based on each topic presented in the graphic organizer.
    b. If they finish early they may begin illustrating their books.
5. Closure
    a. I will ask the children to tell me what perspective is and we will share a journal entry from each group.

Assessment:
Each student will be assessed based on their individual progress throughout the lesson and their individual class work. Students will be assessed based on their performance during class.

Adaptations:
All students will be encouraged to work independently. However, students who are struggling will receive additional support from the teacher. Students who may be having a hard time will be allotted additional time to complete the assignment with the help of the teacher.

Reflection:
This is a very engaging and hands-on lesson that will allow the children to explore fiction and nonfiction literature simultaneously. The children will truly understand what perspective is and how it can be used in writing. I know that this could be a challenge for some students but I also know that this will be a fun and motivating way to push the children to the next level of thinking, in terms of reading and writing. Overall, this lesson was a success!

DIARY OF A FROG

Based on *Diary of a Worm* by Doreen Cronin

June 18th

Mom says there are three things I should always remember:

1. Flies are faster than you think!
2. Don't go too far from the lilly pad.
3. Never trust a bird!

June 23rd

Today my freind toad hoped to my lilly pad. We eat flys and had a great day. I hop toad comes by tamorouw

July 4th

Boom! I fell off my lilly pad when fire poped in the sky. I moved my bolgeing eys around loolig for the birds. They alas trx te eat me. I was so scard.

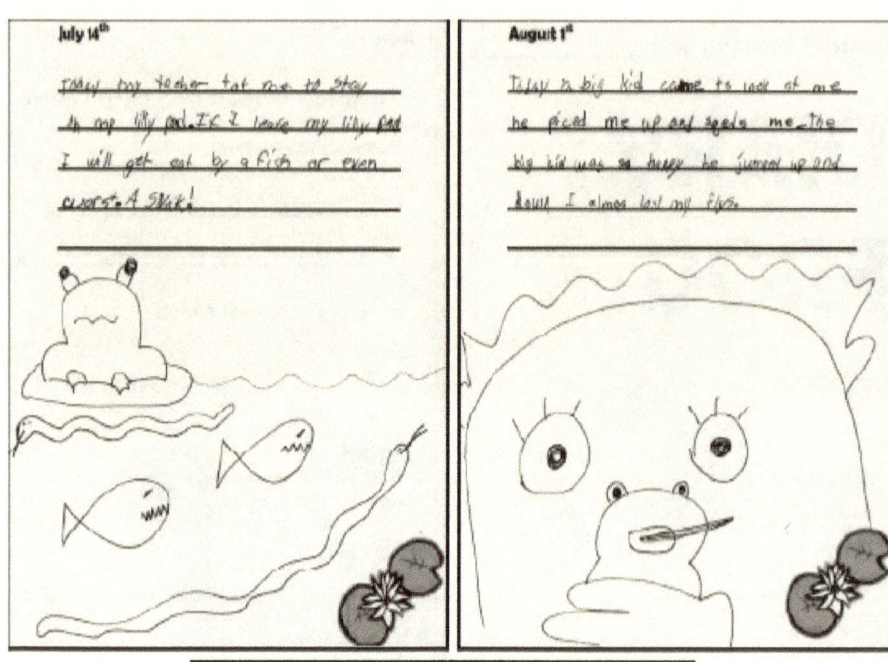

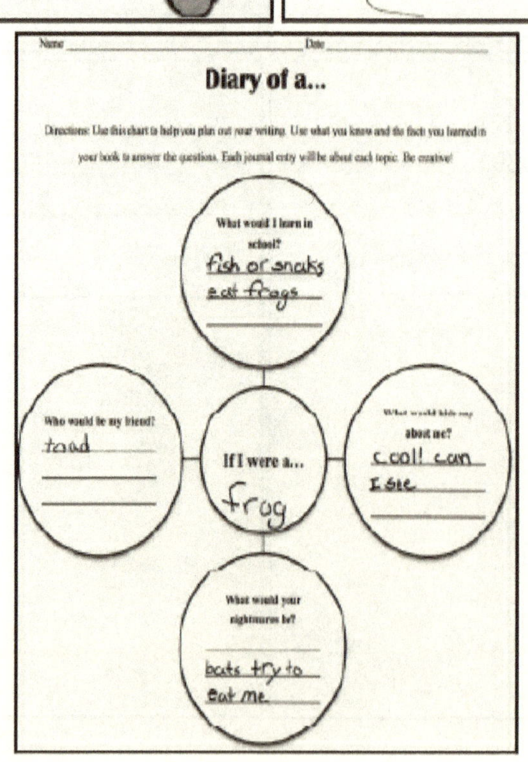

Name ___________________ Date ___________________

Diary of a...

Directions: Use this chart to help you plan out your writing. Use what you know and the facts you learned in your book to answer the questions. Each journal entry will be about each topic. Be creative!

Marisa Landy   3rd Grade Science Lesson

Light and Prism

Lesson Rationale and Context:
I am teaching this lesson as part of our energy unit. The unit focuses on light, sound and heat. We have already taught and conducted experiments with sound and heat. Now, we are focusing on light. Light is energy you can see. The children will learn about the different sources of light. Heat energy and light energy are closely related. The children will learn that light is produced by heat. The class will describe how light moves and the shadows it creates. We will experiment with light prisms to observe the spectrum of light. Next week we will learn about electricity and how we produce light using electricity.

Goal:
The children will identify different light sources and how heat energy and light energy are related.

Objectives:
   Student will be able to:

   1. Identify sources of light.
   2. Explain how heat and light are related.
   3. Tell how light moves and what it creates.
   4. Describe the colors that make up white light.
   5. Apply their knowledge of light to answer questions.
   6. Explain what happens to cause refraction.

NJCCCS:

STANDARD 5.7 (Physics) All students will gain an understanding of natural laws as they apply to motion, forces, and energy transformations.
   B. Energy Transformations

   2. Identify sources of light and demonstrate that light can be reflected from some surfaces and pass through others.

Materials:
   - "Light Energy"
   - Overhead Projector
   - Prisms
   - 2 glass jars
   - 2 pencils
   - Water
   - Flashlights
   - Classroom objects

Anticipatory Set:
Last week, we learned all about heat energy. This week we are learning about light energy. Light and heat energy are very closely related. We know that our main source of heat is from the sun. What is our main source of light? Today, we are doing light centers! We will be experimenting with light in three different ways. First, we need to learn more information about light energy.

Lesson Procedure:

1. Modeling
   a. Today, we will read the book and learn all about light energy.
   b. The booklet introduces the main concepts about light energy. It tells us that light is energy you can see and light mainly comes from the sun. Light also comes from very hot substances and travels in straight lines. It stops when it hits an object. This creates a shadow. When light passes through air to water, it bends. This is called refraction. The bending of the light makes the objects appear to be bent. Refraction occurs when the light slows down as it hits the water. White light is made of many different colors. Prisms are used to separate these colors. Isaac Newton was the first person to prove that white light is made up of different colors

2. Joint Participation
   a. The children will read the booklet aloud.
   b. I will tell the class that we will be doing science centers today.
   c. There are three centers that the children will visit. They will move with a group of 7 children. They will only be given ten minutes to work at each center. Each child must get a turn working at the center. They must remember to work quietly.

3. Guided Practice
   a. The first center is all about prisms. The children will spend a few minutes working at the prism center and answer the questions that go along with this center.
   b. The second center is about refraction. The children will experiment with light passing through air to the water. They can see that the light slows down and causes the object to appear to be bent.
   c. The third center is about shadows. The children will make shadows with flashlights. They will experiment with the direction of the shadow as they move the light source.

4. Independent Work
   a. There will be a set of directions at each center.
   b. The children must follow the directions and answer the questions in their science notebooks

Assessment:
Each student will be assessed based on their individual progress throughout the lesson and their individual class work. Students will be assessed based on their performance during class. At the end of the science unit, the children will be assessed on the concepts of energy.

Adaptations:
All students will be encouraged to work independently. However, students who are struggling will receive additional support from the teacher. Students who may be having a hard time will be allotted additional time to complete the assignment with the help of the teacher.

Evaluation:
The children love science and I know that they will be very excited about this science activity. They also love to be able to move around. They love working within groups and do a very nice job together. This is a class of kinesthetic learners who love science.

Light Energy

Light is energy you can see. Light and heat energy are closely related. Just like with heat energy, our main source of light is the sun. Light can be produced by extremely hot materials.

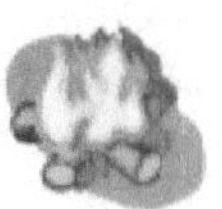

1

When things are very hot, they glow. In fire, there are small burning particles in the flame which glow and produce light. The sun and the stars are huge bodies of very hot gas. The light that comes from our light bulbs is produced by a small hot, glowing wire.

2

Light usually travels in straight lines. This is why shadows are formed. The light stops when it hits the object and cannot continue to move around the object.

3

Shadows can look different depending on where the light is coming from. For example, in the morning, the sun is low. If you are facing the sun, the shadow the light creates will be long and stretched out behind you. At noon, when the sun is at its highest point and almost directly above you, your shadow will be small and very close to your body.

4

When light travels through water, the light rays appear to bend. When you look at an object that is half under water and half above water, it will appear to be bent. This is called refraction.

5

This happens because the light moves at a different speed through the water than it does through the air. Light moves at about 186,000 miles per second through the air! It slows down when it moves through the water. When the light rays slow down, it changes direction.

6

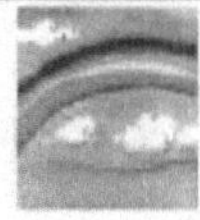

When light enters our atmosphere from the sun it comes as white light. The white light appears white to us, but in reality, it is made up of a number of different colors. When white light enters a prism it separates the colors into the spectrum of light. The colors of the rainbow appear. More than 300 years ago, Isaac Newton, was the first to prove that white light is made up of different colors.

7

Faces have been hidden to respect the privacy of others.

Nubs: Literary Essay

Lesson Rationale and Context: I am teaching this lesson in order to give my special education students a clear understanding of the organizational format of a literary essay. Students will understand how to formulate a clear and strong thesis. They will practice writing a clear, organized and focused literary essay with the help of transitional words and or phrases.

Goal: Each student will successfully write a clear, organized and focused literary essay.

Objectives: Student will be able to:

1. Read and understand the book Nubs.
2. Form a clear and strong thesis about Nubs as a character.
3. Write a clear, organized and focused literary essay.

NJCCCS:
Standard 3.2 (Writing) All students will write in clear, concise, organized language that varies in content and form for different audience and purposes.

3.2.5   B. Writing as a Product (resulting in a formal product or publication)
        9. Provide logical sequence throughout multi-paragraph works by refining   organizational structure and developing transitions between ideas.

3.2.5   D. Writing Forms, Audiences and Purposes (exploring a variety of forms)
        4. Organize a response that develops insight into literature by exploring personal reactions, connecting to personal experiences and referring to the text through sustained use of examples.

Materials:

- Nubs by Major Brian Dennis and Sebastian's Roller Skates by Joan De Deu Prats
- Chart paper, markers, pencils, lined paper, post-its

Day One

Anticipatory Set: I will remind the students of all the prior work we have done within the character unit of reading. As we read I want you to think of character traits that can be used to describe the dog Nubs. The students will listen to the book Nubs as it is read aloud to them. We will mark pages of the book that show Nubs' true character with post-its.

Lesson Procedure:

1. Modeling
   a. Now that we are very familiar with Nubs as a character, we can formulate a thesis for our essay. I can see that throughout the book Nubs is determined. He is determined in many situations and in many ways. I need to make sure my thesis is clear and strong. I can say "Nubs is **determined** even when his survival is at stake." Determination is the character trait that is shown throughout multiple parts of the book. This thesis is clear, direct and strong. I will use a box and bullet graphic organizer to help plan out my essay. My thesis will go into the box. The character trait determination was shown throughout the book and will be repeated and proven throughout my essay.
   b. I will go back to my post-its to find the parts of the book that support my thesis. These parts will strengthen and prove my thesis statement. I will model my thinking about the character Nubs. I will return to the second page and say, "The book says that Nubs is the leader of his pack and that they survived on desert mice, rats and scraps from soldiers. This part makes me think that Nubs is determined to survive despite his living conditions." This is can be my first bullet. I can write "Nubs is the leader of his pack and all they have to eat are desert mice, rats and scraps from soldiers."
2. Joint Participation

a. Now that the children understand how I am formulating my bullets and how my thoughts about his determination are progressing, I will ask them for help in naming the next bullet.
   b. We can return to another part of the book and ask the children to give Nubs a character trait based on his actions here. This part is about Nubs staying with Marine Major Brian on his nightly lookout shift. I will ask the children what this part shows about Nubs' character. We will mark this page with a post-it as well.
   c. Lastly, we will return to the end of the book where Brian must leave Iraq and travel to Jordan. Nubs follows him 70 miles across the desert. I will ask the children what this part shows about Nubs. Does this also show that he is determined? How is Nubs determined here?
3. Guided Practice
   a. Now I will read the book <u>Sebastian's Roller Skates</u> by Joan De Deu Prats aloud to the children. They will follow along with their typed text with post-its ready as they begin to formulate their thesis about Sebastian's character.
4. Independent Work
   a. The children will independently form a thesis that is supported by 3 parts of the text. They will do so in the box and bullet format in their reading journal. As closure, they will share their thesis with their reading/writing partner.

Day Two

Anticipatory Set: I will remind the students of all the prior work we have done within the essay unit of writing. I strong essay has a clear thesis that grows in strength as the essay progresses and ends with a conclusion about your big idea and your own life.

Lesson Procedure:

1. Modeling:
   a. Today I will model how to use the box and bullets we created while reading as an organizer for our writing. My thesis is "Nubs is determined." To make this thesis even stronger I can look at my bullets. I notice that Nubs is often in situations that jeopardize his survival. My revised thesis will be "Nubs is **determined** even when his survival is at stake."
   b. A strong essay with a clear and fluent essay uses transitional phrases in each paragraph and when things are changing throughout the piece. I will create a chart of transitional words and phrases that can be used to make a literary essay stronger and more fluent.
   c. I will model how to write an introduction paragraph using transitional phrases (in blue) to begin my paragraph and my thesis (in orange) in closing my paragraph.
   d. Now I will model how to write the first bullet using transitional phrases (in blue). I will describe what is happening in that part of the book and show how it connects to my thesis. Instead of repeating the thesis again and again, I will teach the children to choose the most important word within the thesis and to repeat that. This will help to strengthen your final repetition of your thesis statement (in orange).
2. Joint Participation:
   a. The children will help me to formulate the next bullet beginning with a transitional phrase (in blue) and ending with our thesis (in orange) proving how this part shows Nubs' determination.
3. Guided Practice:
   a. The children will now draft the final bullet on their own. I will pull them back afterwards and *model* how to conclude the essay using transitional phrases (in blue) and concluding with a lesson I have learned about this character trait.
4. Independent Work:
   a. Now that the students have a clear example of a well written literary essay they will create the final literary essay using their box and bullets as a self-created organizer. They will publish their essay as a finished piece of work.

Assessment: Each student will be assessed based on their individual progress throughout the lesson and their final literary essay. The literary essay will be scored based on a rubric.

Adaptation: This lesson was adapted to my students needs in many ways. The scaffolding and step by step process allowed students to practice a skill until it was mastered. The color coding of words gave importance of the thesis and transitional phrases.

Reflection: This lesson was a great success. The children benefitted from the scaffolding that occurred as the lesson progressed. I have noticed that many of my children are transferring over the box and bullet organizer, transitional phrases and thesis/big word repetition into their writing in preparation for the NJ ASK.

Nubs 🐾

In the book Nubs, there is a dog that lives in Iraq. Nubs is a "dog of war." He was given his name because a terrible person cut his ears down to little nubs. Throughout the book Nubs shows determination even when his survival is at stake.

One part that show this is when Nubs is living in the deserts of an Iraqi warzone. Nubs has to fight for desert rats, mice and scraps from soldiers. With very little to eat, he struggles to survive. This proves that Nubs is determined to survive in awful conditions.

Another part that shows Nubs determination is when he helps Brian. Nubs stays by Brian's side as he works through the night shift to protect the military base. This example shows "Nubs is determined to protect Brian.

Finally, Nubs refused to give up when Brian drove across the country of Iraq to the border of Jordan. Nubs traveled 70 miles through the freezing desert with little food or water. He had to make it across territory ruled by savage wolves and wild dogs. Once again Nubs is determined to remain by Brian's side.

Throughout the book Nubs shows his true nature. Nubs is determined to endure any obstacle that gets in the way of his happiness. In the book, it said "It was a miracle he survived. The bigger miracle may be that this dog of war chose to be a dog of peace." I realize that there are many obstacles in life for all of us. If you want to reach your dreams you must begin with determination. Nubs has taught me to never give up because everything you dream for might be right around the corner, or across the desert!

Sebastian's Roller Skates

By ▮▮▮▮▮

In the book, Sebastian's Roller Skates, there is a kid who doesn't have confidence and always doubts himself on what he can and cannot do. Throughout the book Sebastian does not have confidence. "In the end, he turns the ship around and believes in himself." Having confidence helps you in everything that you do.

One part that shows that is when in the beginning of the book he is blushing and looking at the floor. He also chokes when his teacher asks him a question. By the end of the book he ends up asking a girl out. This shows that Sebastian's confidence is changing him.

Another reason that shows he turns the ship around is when he's dreaming of what his life could be like if he had confidence. For him dreaming of what you want to be like helped him become confident in himself.

Finally Sebastian took his mind off all of his troubles and focused on one thing at a time. For example taking time off troubles helped him build his confidents. Throughout the book Sebastian is trying to find his confidents. Letting his troubles go and focusing on one thing at a time created a new Sebastian that is not shy and who is confident in himself. I realize being confident shows your true colors. Also by showing your confidence you excel in your daily tasks.

Sebastian's Roller Skates

By ███████

In the book, Sebastian's Roller Skates, there is a kid who doesn't have confidence and always doubts himself on what he can and cannot do. Throughout the book Sebastian does not have confidence. "In the end, he turns the ship around and believes in himself." Having confidence helps you in everything that you do.

One part that shows that is when in the beginning of the book he is blushing and looking at the floor. He also chokes when his teacher asks him a question. By the end of the book he ends up asking a girl out. This shows that Sebastian's confidence is changing him.

Another reason that shows he turns the ship around is when he's dreaming of what his life could be like if he had confidence. For him dreaming of what you want to be like helped him become confident in himself.

Finally Sebastian took his mind off all of his troubles and focused on one thing at a time. For example taking time off troubles helped him build his confidents. Throughout the book Sebastian is trying to find his confidents. Letting his troubles go and focusing on one thing at a time created a new Sebastian that is not shy and who is confident in himself. I realize being confident shows your true colors. Also by showing your confidence you excel in your daily tasks.

Sebastian's Roller Skates

By ███████

In the book Sebastian's Roller Skates, Sebastian is a boy who is very shy. Whenever somebody would talk to him he would shrug his shoulders and look down. Throughout the book Sebastian shows me, if you keep trying and don't give up something important will come in handy.

One part of the book that shows this is when, he first found the roller skates he tried but as soon as he stood up he fell right back down. This part shows that he needs practice and if he practices something important will come in handy.

Another part that shows this is when he was walking and he realized that the roller skates were still there and so he tried again and stood up and just fell right back down again. This part shows again that he still needs so more practice to reach his goal.

Finally all the practice came in handy. Since he practiced so much he helped a lady catch her dog. He basically skated across the whole park. Sebastian has finally reached his goal to roller skate. This part shows that if you keep trying you will reach your goal.

Throughout the book Sebastian has shown me if your hard worker some reward will come in handy. In the book Sebastian's Roller Skates even though Sebastian fell "Right on his rear end," he still never gave up. Reading this book made me realize to never give up and reach your goal. This book was really good I'm glad I read it. It tells you an important lesson. NEVER GIVE UP!

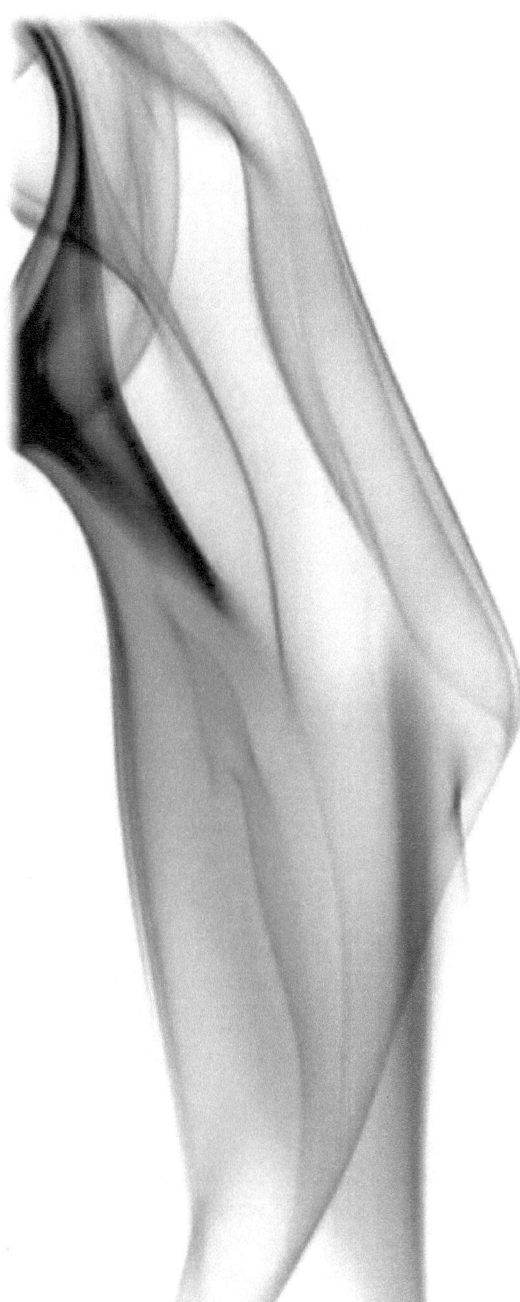

Awakening...
by: John McLeod

Awakening, dawn's chorus
Welcoming,
The day new, untouched
Waiting to be filled....

And will we paint a rainbow
With all its promise
Or dull the canvas
Sadly seen?

Each day brings its own colors'
To be chosen, mixed,
Pigments of joy,
Happy moments,
Smiles and laughter....

And which will you choose?
For 'Life' is choice,
We are all painters
In our own way,
All needing to create
Something of worth,
Of lasting beauty,
Marking our journey....

Footprints in the sand....

The sky today is azure,
The sun warm and golden
A filigree of light and shadow-play
Through the gently swaying trees.

I clean my brushes,
Choose my palette
Of vibrant, living colors,
And begin to fill
Today's blank canvas.

One of the qualities that your mini-portfolio must have is organization. It should also be visually appealing. A cover page and table of contents can be used to address these key qualities.

You can quickly and easily create an attractive cover page in Microsoft Word by clicking "insert" then "cover page" or click "file" then "new," then search for cover page. If you don't see an option that you like, check out the Microsoft website as they have many styles available.

Using a table of contents allows principals to quickly locate the parts of the portfolio that they are most interested in and it shows that you put a lot of thought into organizing your work.

I broke my mini-portfolio down into four categories: application, qualifications, sample lessons, and my philosophy.

In the application section, include your cover letter naming the exact position you'd like and how your experience makes you a great candidate.

The qualification section will hold your resume, copy of certificates, references, and letters of recommendation along with teacher evaluations.

In the sample lesson section, I included three lessons that showed a range of grade levels and areas of curriculum. I also attached actual student work and pictures in one section.

In the philosophy area, I chose to use a poem. It ties my work together and shows my creative side. The poem I chose is about beginning each day with new hope and starting with a clean slate. This is a message I want to give to my students. Most will be intrigued enough to ask why you chose that particular poem, so have an answer ready.

Be prepared to start interviewing the minute you mail out your portfolio. I promise that this is a game changer. If you weren't interviewing before you will definitely be invited in now.

CHAPTER 5: DEDICATE TIME

When you don't have a job, your "job" should be to find one. Spend at least one hour a day looking for open positions in your area. You need to commit to getting hired.

Say it back to me, "I will search for jobs for at least one hour each day." Repeat, "I will search for jobs for at least one hour each day." No, I won't make you write this down a chalkboard but you should really commit to putting this time aside each day. If you don't give yourself the time to look, you're going to miss opportunities. Decide what time of day you're going to designate for your job search and stick with it!

I recommend looking on local newspaper websites in their career opening pages. I also encourage you to look at local district websites because sometimes they won't post listings in the newspaper but they'll have a separate section on their website.

Bookmark county listings of school district websites on your computer. Every week, use the links to see the current openings. If you're really interested in working in a specific district create a separate bookmark and check back multiple times a week. This will only take a few minutes a day but it's a good routine to build.

Immediately after you find a posting, address your cover letter to the specific person listed on the website and prepare to mail the mini-portfolio that same day. It's also productive to research the school and find other administrators who may in charge of hiring and send them their own mini-portfolio. They'll be flattered that you thought of them. When I was hired for my current position, I sent my mini-portfolio to the Director of Special Services who was listed as the contact on the posting, but I also found out the name of the building principal and sent a copy to her.

The more you send, the more chances you have of getting an interview. Diligence and persistence is key.

CHAPTER 6: OPPORTUNITY

Sometimes we can limit ourselves and not even realize that we're doing it. I applied for any and every opening that described the position that I desired, even when I was unfamiliar with the town.

It's ironic- before reading about the open position, I had never heard of the town that I work in now! It's natural to assume that if you've never heard of the town, it must be far away. I'm glad I didn't make that assumption, because you know what they say about those. I applied for the opening because it described the exact type of teaching position I wanted.

I also applied and interviewed at the school I attended when I was young. I wasn't too happy about the idea of working in the town that I was also living in, but I went for it anyway. If it came down to that being my only option, I would've been very happy to take it!

If someone you know has an inside scoop and can help you; go for it. There's no time to hesitate. In my opinion, those who hesitate lose.

If you want something, you have to be ready for it whenever an opportunity shows itself. Isn't that the mindset that we teach our children? As professionals and everyday people we need to be ready for anything.

Take every interview you can, even if it's just an opportunity to practice your interviewing skills.

CHAPTER 7: PRACTICE MAKES PERFECT

You're in luck! On most interviews, you'll be asked many of the same questions. I'm going to go through the most common questions and sample answers. I'll also show you how your mini-portfolio is going to act as your guide during interviews.

Let's talk about some common interview questions that you should memorize and know inside and out. Most principals like to start with, "Tell me a little about yourself." This is a question that may be skipped by principals who have studied your mini-portfolio. They already feel like they know you. However, it's good to practice anyway!

These are the interview questions and answers that I gathered over time and studied before each interview. After each question, I'll give you tips on important details to include when you're formulating your own answers.

Q: Tell me about yourself.

A: Anyone who knows me will tell you that I have a passion for teaching. I discovered this passion during my studies at Montclair State University, majoring in Family and Child Studies with a concentration in early and middle childhood. This major examines the child and the family as a whole, as well as the dynamics of relations and developments.

Last year, I worked full-time, while taking classes, as a para-professional. I worked very closely with two students with special needs. My children were placed in a self-contained first, second and third grade classroom for IRLA and math. They moved to a mainstreamed classroom for science and social studies. My job was to assist them in focusing, developing better social skills, reinforcing concepts and skills, while creating and implementing behavioral plans.

I recently completed my student teaching. During my part-time semester, I worked in a first grade classroom. I also worked in a third grade classroom for a full-time semester. I dedicated my time to the development of my students in both placements. I am the type of person to give it my all in everything that I do. I absolutely love teaching and working with children. Being an educator gives me the opportunity to affect the lives of others in an extremely positive way.

I have been reading <u>The Art of Teaching Reading</u>, by Lucy Calkins, to learn more about reading and writing workshop in an elementary classroom. I am very eager to learn and grow. I know that quality will reflect on my students' performance. I am very resourceful and I will take advantage of any materials that are provided by the district and the community.

Tips: Begin your answer with an outstanding quality that you have and tell how it relates to teaching. Tell about your education, your work experience and the skills that you possess that helped you during that time. Make it clear that you're a lifetime learner who wants to continue to make improvements, either through a Master's Programs, or on your own by listing articles or books that you're reading.

Q: What is your philosophy of education?

A: I believe that all children have the ability to learn and succeed in school. It is the teacher's responsibility to set up a classroom environment in which all children feel safe and secure in order to be ready to learn. Teachers must use various learning styles and intelligences in their lessons to encourage all students to work to their full potential using their strengths as an advantage in their learning. This gives students a chance to use their abilities to improve their skills. It is a teacher's job to support her students' needs.

Tips: Many colleges ask you to write your philosophy of education. If you've written one already, compare that to local school district educational philosophies, especially any districts you're interviewing with.

Q: How would you describe your teaching style?

A: I am a very energetic person and this reflects in my teaching. I am always sure that the children are doing something productive. I make sure that my lessons include student interaction and hands-on activities as much as possible. I believe that students learn best when they are having fun because they are fully involved in the learning process. When children can relate to what they are learning they are also more able to make connections and comprehend new skills and concepts. My teaching style is to have the students actively participate in the learning process.

Tips: Make sure you're telling about your teaching style and infusing your great characteristics that your students love about you.   Your teaching style should make you a strong teacher.

Q: What do you see as your strong points as a classroom teacher?

A: I have a natural ability to connect with many different types of learners. I am able include many different learning styles and multiple intelligences into each of my lessons. I believe that this helps all children to learn at a healthy pace. I am also able to integrate various subject areas into many lessons. This helps my students see connections better. In turn, they are more able to comprehend complex topics and concepts.

Tips: Tell how you will use your own personal and intellectual strengths to improve your teaching.

Q: How do students at your school describe you?

A: My students see me as a young, energetic and caring teacher. They students adore me as I adore them. They see me as the fun teacher who is always doing creative projects, lessons and activities. I am the kind of teacher that will listen to my students' opinions and concerns. I am flexible and like to give my students choices whenever appropriate. I feel that by giving choices students feel respected as individuals and they also have more ownership and accountability within their work.

Tips: Speak from your heart! Tell why the students will love you just as much as adults will.

Q: How would your colleagues describe you?

A: My colleagues would describe me as the tech-savvy, dedicated and very busy new teacher. They will tell you that I am always preparing new lessons and activities that integrate technology. They will also tell you that I am very eager to learn new ideas, strategies and techniques. I'm not afraid to ask questions! I see the importance that this holds. Everyone has something to teach you, it's up to you to be willing to put yourself out there and learn!

Tips: This is a chance for you to show that you're going to be working hard for your classroom and also a people person who will get along well with other teachers. If you're working in a special education position, this is an especially important skill to have.

Q: What is your greatest educational achievement?

A: Thus far, my greatest educational achievement was working closely with a student who was struggling. When this child found a subject difficult, he would display behavioral problems immediately. He would try to avoid work by acting out. I was able to set up a reward system to encourage him to focus and ask for help when he needed it. This child began to show signs of improvement within the first week of the behavioral system being put in place. I am now tutoring him over the summer to help him to keep up with those skills for next year. His parents are very happy with the support that my cooperating teachers and I have given him.

Tips: During student teaching, most of us feel like we've accomplished successes with students. Use an example- show how you recognized a problem and worked to solve it. If you have teaching experience other than student teaching you probably have a long list of achievements. That's the best thing about working with children. Most of them really need the support you can give them and appreciate it more than you know.

Q: What process do you follow to solve problems?

A: I believe that the most important thing to remember when solving problems is communication is key. If you have a problem with anyone- parent, colleague, or student- you need to be sure that the communication is open. You can discuss what the best plan of action is for both sides. It is important to come up with a common goal. This will avoid any other problems from arising and will make it easier for parties to compromise and settle the problem. Many times you can come to a simple agreement leaving both parties happy.

Tips: Here's your chance to show that you're resourceful! In my opinion, having the ability to solve problems is one of the most critical life skills one can possess. Show that you have what it takes.

Q: What do you do for recreation in your classroom?

A: I believe that it is very important for children to have independent reading time. This encourages students to build a love for reading. Research shows that children in classrooms who read for recreation do much better at developing reading skills. I also feel that it is important for students to have options after they have read for a certain period of time. I think that group interaction is important for students to practice even during free time. Games and puzzles are a great way for students to practice group work and also to develop problem solving social skills. I am very interested in setting up centers for my students as well. I feel that centers give students an opportunity to develop skills independently and across the curriculum. Centers can also have different options, allowing for differentiation and various forms of intelligences.

Tips: Use research to back up your answers. It makes your opinions more valid.

Q: In your thinking, what is the most exciting advance in education?

A: Technology in the classroom is growing more and more each year. I am very eager to integrate different means of technology into my classroom. SMART Boards are becoming more and more common in schools in our area. Technology is fun and highly interactive for both teachers and students. Students can better relate to what is going on and are active participants in the learning process. In my opinion, technology should be used whenever possible.

Tips: This is a question that gives you a chance to talk about the exciting new things you'll explore with your students. Make a connection between the exciting advance and how it will improve your students' learning.

Q: What means of communication do you use with your students?

A: It is important for you to have an open relationship with your students. This way, they always know what is expected of them throughout the day. Your students will feel comfortable in your classroom and build a strong rapport with you. I feel that the classroom environment is very closely related to how well your students will perform. If a child is uncomfortable, he or she cannot focus on the learning process. When a child is comfortable to express himself, he or she can work to their full potential.

Tips: This is another opportunity to show that you're easy to work with and you communicate well. Students and parents will enjoy being around you. Communication is a pertinent skill to master when teaching.

Q: What do you consider the teacher's biggest pressure?

A: I believe that a teacher's biggest pressure is to make sure that each student is learning to the best of their ability. A teacher must be able to juggle a mixture of levels and learning styles to ensure that each student's needs are being supported. By teaching to many different types of learning styles and intelligences, you allow each student to use their strengths to support and strengthen their weaknesses.

Tips: Pressure and stress are an unavoidable part of life. Tell how you'll overcome or deal with the biggest pressures of teaching.

Q: What is your educational goal?

A: My biggest educational goal is to give each student the opportunity and the encouragement to work to their full learning potential. Another goal is to ensure that all students' needs are being met. There are many different ways for me to meet these goals. I believe that teaching to many different learning styles and multiple intelligences, is one way to ensure the opportunity of growth and development for all students.

Tips: State your goal and how you'll work to achieve it.

Q: How do you differentiate in your lessons?

A: It is important to remember that all children learn differently so differentiation is key. I use formative assessments to determine how and when to differentiate. I can quickly see which students would benefit from differentiating the lesson.

To make sure that you reach each of your students in all of your lessons, it is vital to incorporate many types of intelligences and learning styles. I include many hands-on activities for the bodily-kinesthetic learners. I give my students a chance to work in groups for interpersonal intelligences and also an opportunity for students to reflect independently for the interpersonal and the logical learners. I also supply my students with many visual aids for the spatial learners. I always include a small writing activity connected to my science lessons as well for the learners who were verbal-linguistic. We close all of our lessons with a class discussion where children developed their problem-solving skills and also were able to make real-life connections to the things that we learned. This gives all students the opportunity and encouragement to support all levels and needs.

In order to differentiate effectively, you must first get to know your students and what their needs are. You can do so by reviewing notes from previous years and IEP's, whenever possible. You also need to observe your students to see what their learning styles are, as well as weaknesses and strengths. Once you know your students' style you can try different approaches to see what works best. What works for one student will not work for all students. Now that you know the students well, you will know how to differentiate for their needs.

I differentiated for one student every day by reinforcing the big ideas of the lesson one-on-one after whole class instruction. He was a kinesthetic learner and he used a lot of manipulatives to understand concepts. We worked together day after day until he understood the process. I am currently tutoring him so that he can continue to build upon these skills over the summer.

Tips: In my opinion, this is a question should require your process for determining the types of student that you have and providing examples of how and when you would differentiate.

Q: How would you handle a sticky situation with colleagues?

A: Communication is the most important aspect of solving any problem. I am a very open and understanding person. I feel that almost any problem can be solved just by talking about it. It is always important to respect differences in opinion, especially in our diverse society. If you can agree on a common goal, the problem solving process becomes much easier for both parties.

Tips: Principals want to hear that you have respect for others and the ability to manage problems well.

Q: How would you handle a problem with a parent?

A: Just as with a problem with a colleague, communication is the answer. I have an open-door policy with parents so that they feel comfortable voicing their concerns.   I believe that the most important thing to express to a parent is that you both have the same goal in mind. You both want their child to learn and perform to the best of their ability. This will help to put their mind at ease and from there you can discuss the problem and develop a plan to solve it. Parents appreciate hearing that you care about their child and that you're looking out for their best interests as well.

Tips: Most principals will ask a lot about handling problems. Teachers must show respect for others as well as demonstrate tact in unsettling positions or circumstances.

Q: What classroom management systems will you put into action?

A: From day one, I will let my students know what is expected of them. I will ask the children on the first day of school what they want their classroom to be like. We will discuss what rules should be put in place to keep our classroom that way. Together, we will create a list of rules and students will sign their names to show that they agree with them. This way, each child will feel confident that they had an active role in determining the classroom rules. They will be more opt to understand why the rules are in place and have more ownership over following them.

I will have a turn-card system in place as well. I will explain to the children that they will each have a card with their name on it. If their card is green, they are having a great day. It they have a yellow card, they need to slow down and think about their actions and what they should be doing differently. If they have a red card, they need to stop what they are doing and decide what needs to be done to correct their behavior. This will result in a conference with the teacher and a phone call to their parents.

I believe that positive reinforcement is the best form of classroom management. Once students see that only positive behavior will be rewarded, they will learn to act in an appropriate manner. Students who are caught doing the right thing will be rewarded with praise on a normal basis.

Tips: It's good to express that you'll give students clear expectations and involve them in making the rules. This way they'll have ownership over them. If you do all the work, then you'll own the outcome, not your students.

Q: How will you structure your reading program?

A: I will have a classroom library that is organized by reading level and genre. Students will be given independent reading time throughout the day. I believe that it is important for students to have choices when it comes to independent reading. They should read about what they are interested in. This approach helps students explore and find areas of reading that they love.

After an initial assessment of their reading ability, they will be placed in leveled reading groups. I will be sure to give clear expectations of rules of the reading groups. Students will be supported in holding productive conversations about their books. I will inform the students that the groups will change as the year goes on and as we all become better readers. I will encourage children to use strategies when reading including looking at pictures and sounding out words, and using the text to support their thinking.

Tips: Use tips that you learned from student teaching and commonly used reading programs.

Q: How will you structure your writing program?

A: I will be sure to allow students to write about what they know. They will be encouraged to use pictures to illustrate their ideas and elaborate on their ideas. I will always ask them to tell me about their work. This enables further thinking skills. The children will share their work with their peers as well. I will compliment what parts of writing they're doing well and I'll ask them questions about their writing to see how they can improve it. I will also encourage them to edit their work and their peer's work. I will also encourage them to revisit work that they have completed so that they can continue to develop their skills and ideas.

Tips: Show that regardless of the program you're going to reach all types of learning styles and intelligences.

Q: Why should I recommend you for this position?

A: I am a very dedicated individual and I have a true passion for teaching. I know that I have what it takes to make an outstanding teacher. I have very strong communication skills and I am eager to learn. I work well with children, parents and teachers alike, as I am a team player. I will be an asset to this learning community, as I will take an active role in promoting student development.

Tips: Tell what makes you the best choice! List the key skills that you possess that will make you an asset to the school and community.

Q: Why did you decide to be a teacher?

A: I have a natural ability to connect with children. I believe that teaching gives you an opportunity to impact the lives of your students in an extremely positive way. Teaching allows you to be an active member in a community. Teaching is also very rewarding.

Tips: Be honest and show off your qualities at the same time.

These were the answers that I rehearsed aloud and modified to include details that I knew were important to the school district I was interviewing with. Obviously, they match my experiences and opinions. They will need to be modified to apply to your feelings, experiences and knowledge.

I cannot express enough how important it is to type up written answers and recite your answers out loud. You can't forget them that way. Think of it as a form of studying. When you want to commit something to long term memory it helps to read it, write it, say it and repeat it.

Everyone gets nervous; it's a sign that you care! However, getting too nervous can make it difficult to remember your answers. That's why you need to rehearse before getting an interview, the day of the interview and then reflect after interviewing. Was your answer even better than planned when you were in the interview? Great! Write it down. Practice makes perfect.

Now, let's get to the best part. Having sent a mini-portfolio prior to your interview, the principal already has the answers to many of those questions. Your mini-portfolio is going to be a guide for your interview. It's going to direct the conversation and you'll be able to point to physical examples of the qualities you want the interviewer to recognize in you. It gives you credibility and makes it easy for a principal to visualize you in their school.

Back in June of 2011 when I was interviewed for my current position I had used my mini-portfolio to set the stage for my interview.

Upon my arrival, the Director of Special Services said to me, "It's so nice to meet you. I'm so happy to finally put a face to your name!"

I couldn't have expected a better introduction. It shows the impact that my mini-portfolio had made. I had an opportunity to make a first impression before even being invited in for an interview.

CHAPTER 8: FORGET THE RULES!

Seriously! Forget the rules! Don't be afraid to take risks. Without risk, there's no reward.

If I followed the rules, I wouldn't have gotten noticed. I would have continued to blend in with the rest of the plain, boring, paper resumes.

Here are some rules that you'll hear about and the reasons why I believe it's acceptable to break them.

Rule: Your resume can't be any longer than one page.

Why not? I wouldn't go any longer than one doubled sided page, but if your experience is more than what can fit onto a single-sided page, more power to you. I do feel that it needs to be structured to show that you are an organized individual-super important when teaching- but it can definitely be double sided with adjusted font size and margins.

Rule: After interviewing, don't call until a week has passed or don't call to follow-up at all, just wait to hear back.

What? This sounds like a dumb dating rule too! Sometimes, it's healthy to break the rules and just go against the grain. It shows that you're interested and you're eager. I wouldn't call the next day, but if you interviewed on a Tuesday, it's perfectly acceptable to call on Friday.

Rule: Only send digital applications and don't bother with mailing a paper copy or mini-portfolio, especially when the district says so.

Most school districts want you to fill out a digital application. I recommend you do that and then some. In this situation, doing more gets you more recognition. A supervisor can choose not to open your mini-portfolio but, I guarantee you that if it makes it to their desk they're going to open it. We're going to make it so appealing that they won't be able to resist. It will catch their immediate attention.

PART 2: I GOT AN INTERVIEW! NOW WHAT?

CHAPTER 9: RESEARCH & INVESTIGATE

Research the school and the school district before every interview. There are three simple and easy ways to find information about a school district. One is through the school website, another is by Googling the school district and the last is by talking to people you may know who works in the district or even live in the town.

When looking at the district website, you'll want to examine these areas: district philosophy, superintendent's message, district curriculum, the specific school website, principal's message and a sampling of teacher webpages.

The district philosophy is something you'll want to know before interviewing. Some principals may ask you, "How does your educational philosophy fit into our school philosophy?" You'll want to prepare for this by noticing the key points of the district philosophy.

The superintendent's message is very telling about the atmosphere of the school and district. Most likely, if your interview with the principal goes well, you'll interview with the superintendent next.

The district curriculum will help you to determine which math and language arts programs the school uses. Usually, principals want to know that you're experienced using the programs that the school uses or that you've done some reading about the program. If you're unfamiliar with the programs-research them. This shows that you're resourceful and you can solve problems.

Be prepared to answer questions about how you'll implement their math, reading and writing programs in your classroom. Many teachers post YouTube videos and create Pinterest boards all about how they use various reading, writing and math programs in their classrooms. This is a great way to learn about the programs and see examples of how other teachers are using them with students every day.

You can also check out teachers' webpages who currently work at the school. This will give you an idea of some of the school's events and the atmosphere of the school. I would look at the teachers in the grade level that you're interviewing for and see what they're doing. Most teachers are required to update their webpages every month or so. This will give you a good idea of what you'll be doing as well.

If you haven't had much luck with the school website, Google the school to see what information you can find. Each school has a "Report Card" which lists statistical information, such as test scores and the economic standing of the school population. You may also find articles written about current events happening in the school or the school district. This will be useful information to know during your interview.

Now that you've done your homework, you'll want to use that to your advantage. Customize your interview questions and answers to match the school and district. Make the principal feel confident that what you don't know you'll work to figure out. I recommend that you recite your customized interview answers aloud to ensure confidence under pressure.

CHAPTER 10: INTERVIEW TIPS & POINTERS

I'm going to share all of the tips and pointers I've gathered over the years. If you follow these tips, your interview will go smoother and hopefully you'll avoid any awkward moments!

Tip # 1: Be friendly with the secretary!

I made it a point to sit in a chair that was closest to the secretary's desk when I was waiting for the interview to begin. Most secretaries are friendly and will say hello to you upon entering. Use this as an opportunity to initiate conversation. Compliment her- in a genuine way of course! Or say something nice you've heard about the school if that seems more natural. Trust me when I say, most principals are very close with their secretaries. It's very likely that they ask their opinion of the candidates or the secretaries just offer their opinion. This is true, especially if they get a great impression of you.

Tip # 2: Be an active listener!

This means you should be practicing good conversational skills and keep track of the topics that the principal is stressing most. These topics reveal areas that the principal values. You can learn a lot about the principal and the school just by listening carefully. This information will be very helpful if and when you're invited in for a demonstration lesson.

Tip # 3: Ask meaningful questions.

I recommend looking at the website before interviewing so you can prepare a question as well. Most principals will end the interview by saying, "do you have any questions for me?" Sometimes it's hard to think of something on the spot. A meaningful question might be about community events or character building programs. You can express how important you feel it is for the community to be involved with the school or how significant it is for students to learn how to build character. This shows that you care about people and that's meaningful!

Tip # 4: Don't be afraid to say you don't know the answer to a question but you'd love to learn about it.

If a principal asks you about Reading Workshop and you don't know what it is, it's good to say, "I don't have experience in that program yet, can you tell me what it's like?" This is the perfect opportunity to ask a meaningful question. Once the principal tells you about the program, this is your chance to tell what you do know about similar programs. You can also show that you're resourceful and motivated to learn more. Ask the principal if she can recommend any reading that will help you catch up on the topic. If you ask the right questions when you're unsure of an answer, you can turn something that may initially seem negative into a positive.

Tip # 5: Remember to smile!

We all get nervous during interviews but teachers are supposed to be friendly, especially under pressure. No child likes a teacher that brings personal business and feelings into her classroom or shows that they're stressing over standardized testing. You want your principal to visually see that you handle pressure well. This is another reason why you need to practice, practice, practice!

PART 3: AFTER THE INTERVIEW

CHAPTER 11: PLEASE AND THANK YOU

After interviewing, send a genuine, handwritten thank you note. Put it in the mail that same day.

You want your interviewer to have something that'll remind them of you. Most likely it will sit on their desk for a few days. I don't recommend emailing a thank-you note because it could get lost with all of their other emails. My principal says she gets one hundred or more emails a day. You want to make sure what you send is tangible and handwritten. It shows that you care and that you're eager to hear back from her.

Here is a sample thank you note that you can adjust to meet your needs.

Dear __________,

Thank you for giving me the time to meet with you. I enjoyed our conversation. I know that if given the opportunity, I will truly be an asset to your school. I look forward to hearing from you soon.

Sincerely,

____

It's short and sweet, but shows that you're serious about the opportunity. Make sure you send a thank you card to everyone who attends the interview. You want the supervisors to know that you're going to make sure that students in the school have good manners because it's important to you as well.

CHAPTER 12: CONTINUE THE PROCESS

Did you ever hear the phrase don't put all of your eggs in one basket? Well it's a cliché, because it's true!

You may have done fantastic on your interview, with your dream principal, in your dream position, but it's never smart to count on it. Think of the story of the tortoise and the hare. The hare was so set on winning that he was bold enough to nap while the perseverance of the tortoise defeated him.

Your time will not be wasted if you interview elsewhere and you wind up getting the job you wanted anyway. You'll only be gaining valuable experience and more confidence.

Do not rest until you've signed a contract!

PART 4: EXPECT A DEMONSTRATION LESSON

CHAPTER 13: BELLS & WHISTLES

If you've done well in your interview, you should expect to be invited in for a demonstration lesson. This is standard procedure; unless a principal needs to make a fast decision.

Bring all of your bells and whistles. Once you have the job, principals want to see what you would do on an ordinary day when they come in to observe you. However, at a demonstration lesson, you set the stage to make your lesson the most appealing for students, the teacher and the principal.

When you're invited in for the demonstration lesson, ask the principal how much time you'll have and if you can have the teacher's email address. That way, you can ask the teacher for the number of students, if there are any disabled students-who require modifications- and for a list of names so you can make them name tags. An interactive lesson is only effective if everyone knows everyone's name! If you want students to work in groups, ask the teacher to help you create the groups through email or upon your arrival. He or she knows which students will work best together.

I would use technology in some way because it's almost a guarantee to catch the students' interest that way. If the students seem bored and aren't engaged, the principal won't be impressed.

When I gave my demonstration lesson, my principal had told me that she wanted a 40 minute writing lesson. I asked for the teacher's email address so that I can run the ideas past her. She was more than happy to help answer my questions. I asked what technology she had available in her room, the number of students and what modifications she was currently responsible for as the special education teacher.

From my research, I knew that the school used Teachers College Reading Writing Workshop. I wanted to use this information to my advantage and I also wanted to hook the students with technology.

I wrote a simple sentence telling the students that it described a movie character that I was sure everyone in the class knew. However, the sentence lacked important detail that would let my audience know who I was referring to. When I asked the students if they knew who the character was, of course, no one knew. I pretended to be shocked and showed them a video clip from Finding Nemo. The class immediately told me that I didn't describe the character well enough.

I used a chart to list words that show (not tell) how something looks, sounds, feels, taste and/or smells. Students helped me to infuse more detail into my sentence so that it became easier to understand and clear who and what it was describing.

Students worked independently to revise another bland sentence from a different part of the movie. While watching that scene from the movie and students listed details on their organizer. Then they worked on making the sentence more I circulated and supported them. I closed the lesson by asking students if they can tell me why using details are important. Almost every special education child raised their hand and shared their answer to show that they understood.

Don't be nervous if you see other teachers are giving a lesson that same day. Usually districts are required to invite three candidates in for a demo and in my district, they try to schedule all three demonstrations for the same day!

Be confident, positive and prepared. You want the principal, the teacher and the students to remember you. You want to leave with the students smiling.

CHAPTER 14: THINK OUTSIDE THE BOX

Think outside of the box when planning your demonstration lesson! You don't want to do something generic and risk having the next person do the same, except maybe better. This is your chance to show just how creative you can be.

Gather interactive, fun and diverse ideas from teaching blogs, Pinterest and other social media sites. This will help you greatly during your lesson planning and help you to stand out from the others.

Make yourself stand out! You goal should be to give a memorable performance for the supervisors observing and for the children participating.

PART 5: AFTER A JOB OFFER

CHAPTER 15: BOARD APPROVAL

As I mentioned in Chapter 12, do not rest until you've signed a contract! Oh and I forgot to mention, don't rest until your contract has been board approved.

In most cases, getting Board approval is a simple formality, but you never know. I've heard stories of things going terribly wrong at the very last minute. It's smart to protect yourself in the worst case scenario.

This is why I recommend going on interviews until you've been board approved. I continued interviewing and even did a demonstration lesson when I was awaiting my board approval at my current position. Even though I didn't sign with those districts, it gave me security in knowing that I wasn't limiting myself if the worst case scenario did occur. Either way, I would have a job.

CHAPTER 16: COMPARE DISTRICTS

If you've been given multiple job offers, you'll want to compare the position and the district. Ask yourself, which position can I best see myself in? Which school community best matches your needs? Will I be happy here in the long run?

One way to determine if this is the district for you is by looking up the district contracts online and compare salaries. Teacher salaries are considered public information so this should be easy to find. Sometimes you won't find the current year's salary guide, but you should be able to find a fairly recent guide.

I was given offers at 5 competitive districts. In order to make the best decision possible, I made a chart that compared the contract details.

The chart showed the starting salary and the salaries at Step 5, 10 and the top. It was easy to see that some districts started out high and then ended low. You want to be in a district that's going to start moderately and progress to a high ending salary because that's what your pension is built on.

Something else to consider is longevity. This means that over time you'll earn your salary and an additional percentage based on the contract and the years you've put in.

Use the chart to compare the starting, middle and ending salaries. Most public salary guides will provide you with information about longevity, days off, and perhaps even benefits.

I hope that by using these tools, the process of getting the teaching job you desire comes naturally and with ease.

CONCLUSION

I hope that this book inspires you to go after your dreams with more power than ever before.

One of my greatest role models, Walt Disney once said, "All our dreams come true, if we have the courage to pursue them."